RUTH FIELDING
AT GOLDEN PASS

ALICE B. EMERSON

Ruth Fielding #22

0

WILDSIDE PRESS

RUTH FIELDING AT GOLDEN PASS

ALICE B. EMERSON

Ruth Fielding #22

WILDSIDE PRESS

Originally published in 1925.
Published by Wildside Press, LLC.
Visit us online at wildsidepress.com.

CHAPTER 1

FIRE

Main Street was jammed with an unprecedented crowd of people and traffic. Automobiles discharged a continual stream of humanity before the doors of the new motion picture house in Cheslow.

Laughing girls and their escorts, older men and women, paused before the rather flamboyant poster in the lobby of the picture house advertising Miss Ruth Fielding's personal appearance with the introduction of this, her new and greatest picture, "Snowblind."

Nearly all Cheslow had turned out in honor of this star in picturedom, Ruth Fielding. As Ruth had been a resident of Cheslow since her childhood, it is not strange that the town took a proprietary interest in her.

At that particular moment poor Ruth was feeling extremely unlike the Miss Fielding of the flamboyant poster. She was excited and nervous, and the prospect of facing such an audience as would in all probability pack the Palace that night filled her with an emotion akin to panic.

Also, though she was sure in her own mind that *Snowblind* was a good picture, felt that she had put the best of her art into the making of it, there was always the doubt as to just how it would be received by that fickle thing, an American audience.

The latter, besides being fickle, was pitiless. Where it condemned, it condemned so heartily that the object of its displeasure might just as well be sent at once to the darkest corner of the director's room of discarded plays. It was done for—a complete failure. This, unless there was the possibility of practically remaking the whole thing. And in the case of Ruth Fielding's "Snowblind," where the scenes had actually been filmed amid the snow and ice of the far North, retakes would be an impossibility.

Some of this Ruth had been saying to her chum, Helen Cameron, as she restlessly paced the length of the living room at the Red Mill. The two girls were dressed and ready to start for the theater, but were awaiting the arrival of Tom, Helen's twin brother, and Helen's fiancé, Chess Copley, who were to take them to their destination in Tom's car.

"Helen, if my picture doesn't go and go big," said Ruth, pausing in her restless pacing to stare at her chum, "I think I shall die of disappointment."

Helen laughed. There was a light in her eye as though she enjoyed a secret all her own. She seated herself, unnoticed by her chum, in a chair by the window from which she could command a view of the approach to the Red Mill.

"Cheer up, Ruthie," she said. "Disappointment seldom kills." Then, as she drew forth a pocket mirror and carefully examined her nose for a hint of shine, she added: "Anyway, your 'Snowblind' hasn't a chance in the world to fail, Ruth Fielding. It is a tremendous picture, and you know it."

"If only the public will think so, too!" said Ruth, half to herself. She went over to the window and looked out impatiently. "Isn't it time for the boys to come?"

"Gracious me, so it is!" cried Helen, with a glance of mock surprise at her wrist watch. "These laggards shall suffer for such neglect. Wait till I get hold of Chess—"

"Don't rave. Here comes some one now," Ruth interrupted.

Still enjoying her secret, Helen attempted to get Ruth away from the window. But the latter had seen something which roused her curiosity and she would not be moved.

"What do you suppose that means?" she asked herself, puzzled. "There's more than one car. Why, it's a regular procession—one, two, three! Helen, you know, you bad child!" She turned to her chum, caught the mischievous gleam in her eyes, and shook her a little impatiently. "Tell me! What is it?"

For answer, Helen held up a warning hand.

"Listen!" she said.

Across the still night air, there came a sound of singing.

> "Sweetbriars come here, one by one,
> But one wide river to cross!
> There's lots of work, but plenty of fun,
> With one wide river to cross!
>
> Sweetbriars all-l!
> One wide river of Knowledge!
> Sweetbriars all-l!
> One wide river to cross!"

There was an instant's hush. Then before Ruth could move from where she stood spellbound, the old yell crashed through the silence.

> "S.B.—Ah-h-h!
> S.B.—Ah-h-h!
> Sound our battle-cry

6

Near and far!
S.B.—All!

Briarwood Hall!
Sweetbriars, do or die—
This be our battle-cry—
Briarwood Hall!
That's all!"

It was a full second after the magic of that yell had died away into the silence of the evening before Ruth could command herself to action.

Then with a stifled cry she darted out to the porch.

A whirlwind met her, a whirlwind of bear-like hugs and joyful greetings.

"Ruthie, don't say we actually surprised you!"

"Here, get away, Ann Hicks! I haven't had my chance at her yet."

"Let go of her, Heavy! There won't be enough left to speak its piece tonight!"

These and other gay and jumbled greetings half-deafened Ruth. She pushed the surprise party away from her in an effort to identify more clearly the members of it. Happy tears sprang to her eyes as she recognized them all.

"Nettie Parsons, you old dear. Give me another hug, that's the girl. Bless me! There's The Fox, as large as life and twice as natural. And Mercy Curtis! How well you look, honey! All the dear old crowd. Heavy," she turned accusingly to the rather large young woman who hovered in the background of the group, "are you responsible for this?"

"Not guilty! Ask Ann—she knows!"

There were young men in the party, too, friends of Tom and Chess, whom the latter had asked to play escort to Ruth's old school chums who had come on to Cheslow at the instigation of Mrs. Jennie Marchand, nee Stone, and Ann Hicks.

Ruth knew these boys and nodded to them pleasantly enough. But she was still too taken up with the delightful and unexpected arrival of these old friends of hers to accord the male members of the party much attention.

The latter followed the girls back into the house, grinning indulgently at the clatter of tongues and the happy exclamations of the reunited chums.

"I must sit down! The surprise has been too much for me!" Ruth laughed as she sank down on the couch and the girls clustered on every side of her. "Now tell me, Jennie Marchand or Ann Hicks, or whoever is responsible, just how it happened."

"Ann started the ball rolling," responded Jennie Marchand, she of the round face and jolly smile. "Conceived the bright idea of getting some of the Briarwood Hall girls together—some of the old crowd, who had helped make 'Heart of a School Girl' famous—justly famous, I may say—"

"So," Ann Hicks continued eagerly, "we gathered together as many of the old guard as we could at such short notice and—here we are."

"Yes, here you are!" cried Ruth, looking about at them affectionately. "And now, if no one objects, I think I shall start at the beginning and hug you all over again!"

This pleasing ceremony being satisfactorily accomplished, Tom stepped forward with the suggestion that they start for the theater at once.

"Oh, is every one going?" asked Ruth, innocently enough. For the moment she had actually forgotten her picture.

"Is every one going? Just hear the child!" Jennie Marchand—affectionately known in the old days as "Heavy"—stood with arms akimbo regarding Ruth amusedly. "May I ask, Ruth Fielding, what you think we came all the way to Cheslow for?"

"Besides seeing you!" said Mercy Curtis in Ruth's ear. Mercy did not live far away.

"More than that," declaimed Mary Cox, more popularly known in schooldays as "The Fox," "we have prepared a delectable spread for you after the show, Ruth Fielding, to celebrate the success of 'Snowblind'."

Uncle Jabez Potter and Aunt Alvirah appeared at the moment and attention was instantly turned to them. Most of the girls had met Aunt Alvirah, who greeted them with a fluttering cordiality.

Uncle Jabez acknowledged the introductions in his usual crabbed fashion and declared that if they did not start at once they would be late for the show.

"The picture'll be over before we get there," he grumbled. "And us with a chance to stay home and make ourselves comfortable."

"Cheerful old boy," whispered Jennie Marchand in Helen's ear. "Face like a nut cracker."

Helen looked toward Uncle Jabez and grimaced ruefully.

"He never approved of Ruth's interest in the pictures," she said. "If he had had his way Ruth would never have gone much farther than the Red Mill."

"And look at her now!" said Nettie Parsons.

"Yes, look at her now," laughed Helen. "Our old schoolmate, Ruth Fielding, is on the way to becoming quite a personage, I'll have you know!"

There were a great many others who, either publicly or privately, echoed that view on this particular evening. For the showing of *Snowblind* was a sweeping triumph from the preliminary scenes taken in New York to those final tremendous and climatic scenes taken in the snow-blanketed and wind-swept spaces of the frozen North.

The story held together from start to finish, a proof of Ruth's ability both as scenario writer and director. Anita Townsend and Grand, the co-stars of the picture, were almost equally fine in their portrayal of the parts assigned them, while the introduction of the old trappers gave just the necessary added touch of local color.

The audience wept—and this included most emphatically Ruth's school chums—when author and actors demanded it, laughed at their will, and applauded thunderously the dramatic scenes. In the inspiration of their enthusiasm Ruth forgot her reluctance to speak in public. Instead, she was eager to meet this friendly and appreciative audience.

At the close of the picture she stepped upon the stage and into the spotlight. Her young voice came to them clearly, holding them tense and interested as she related the adventures of her party in the frozen country, described how the various "locations" were found and the pictures filmed.

"Doesn't our Ruthie look too sweet for words, Heavy? Aren't you proud of her?" whispered Helen.

"Yes, surely. But listen to her!"

"And now," Ruth finished, "I want to thank you all in behalf of my company and myself for your appreciation and your generous applause. We all —"

A sharp explosion caught up her words, drowning them in a fierce detonation. From here and there in the audience rose frightened cries.

"The theater is on fire!"

"Fire! fire! The theater is on fire!"

"Let me get out of this!"

"I'll be burnt to death! Oh!"

CHAPTER 2

TOM TO THE RESCUE

As the panic-stricken cries were rising terrifyingly in the over-crowded theater pandemonium was intensified by the sudden blinking out of all the lights.

To be frightened when one can see what danger threatens is one thing. To be frightened in the dark is quite another!

Confusion became panic. Voices already raised in protest or entreaty became shrill or hoarse with fear. Mothers called to their children, children cried for their mothers. The shouts of men rose, entreating those in their charge to "sit tight and not get scared"—as though they were not pretty well scared themselves, if they would but admit it!

At the sound of the explosion Ruth had gone as calmly as she could from the stage to the little bare room that was all there was "behind the scenes" of the theater.

In the darkness she was forced to feel her way. Suddenly a cloud of smoke descended upon her, engulfed her, wrapped her about, almost smothering her. She raised her head instinctively to draw in a breath of fresh air and found there was no fresh air in that stifling place.

Really frightened now, gasping and sputtering, she floundered about in the dark, stumbling over things, aware that others were desperately seeking escape.

"If Tom would only come!" she cried to herself. "I can't find the door—there isn't any door—this awful smoke—oh, if Tom would come!"

She thought of her friends back there in the well of the theater—thought of Aunt Alvirah and groaned.

She had not the slightest doubt but what Tom was trying to find her. He would get to her if such a thing were possible. But that smoke—impossible to breathe—

Tom was doing his best. Out in the dark well of orchestra seats was a living, surging nightmare. Some had succeeded in making their way to the exits, had escaped from the smoke-filled exterior to the blessed fresh air.

But there were those who sought, desperately, friends or members of their families who had become separated from them in the darkness and panic.

Ruth's own party was among these. The boys gripped the girls to prevent their being carried into the aisles by the maddened crowds that swept past them. Chess had found Helen and was urging her to sit quietly.

"The only danger is being caught in the mob," he shouted. "Let these people get out first."

"But Ruth!" Helen gasped. "She may be trapped there behind the stage!"

"Tom will take care of her," Chess prophesied confidently. "Tom— where is Tom?"

He felt in the seat beside him where just a few moments before Helen's brother had been sitting and found, not Tom, but some alien person who growled at him and pushed past in the general rush to the exits.

At that moment a feeble form brushed against him, a bony old hand clutched at his arm.

"Ruth!" gasped the harsh voice of Uncle Jabez Potter. "Somebody's got to get ahold o' that girl!"

Chess put an arm about the old man's shoulders to steady him.

"It's all right," he managed to gasp through the thick cloud of smoke that rolled down upon them. "Tom will see to her."

"Where's Aunt Alvirah?" It was Jennie Marchand's voice shouting through the dark. "You've got to find her, you boys!"

"I'm here!" quavered an old voice, reassuringly close by. "But it don't matter about me. Somebody go find my pretty."

At that very moment Tom was battling his way to the stage. He called Ruth's name wildly over and over while he fought the smoke and acrid fumes to the space behind the scenes.

As for Ruth, though she had faced many and varied dangers before, just now all of them seemed trifling to the one she was passing through.

Her adventurous career had dated from that time when, as an orphan of twelve, she had come to live with Great-uncle Jabez Potter and his sweet, eccentric housekeeper, Aunt Alvirah Boggs.

The Red Mill was just outside the town of Cheslow. In the first volume of the series, entitled "Ruth Fielding of the Red Mill," Ruth had become acquainted with Tom Cameron. The boy had been fortunate enough to do the orphan a service and it was through Tom that she had met his twin sister Helen. Mr. Cameron was a rich widower and business man and lived with his two children in a rather imposing mansion about a mile from the Red Mill.

A short time after her arrival at her new home Ruth was able to save Uncle Jabez a considerable amount of money. In return for this she was allowed by the old man to enter the boarding school, Briarwood Hall, in company with Helen Cameron. It was at this time that Ruth's adventures really began.

At school and college she made many friends, among them Jennie Stone, who had later married Henri Marchand, a distinguished Frenchman.

While still at school, Ruth became interested in the work of scenario writing, and in that work achieved a fair success from the start.

The group of her friends who had planned the surprise party on this particular occasion in order to see the first showing of *Snowblind* had all taken part in Ruth's early scenario, entitled "The Heart of a Schoolgirl," in which Ruth herself had played the part of chum to the heroine, a part taken by a woman already known on the screen. From that time on all Ruth's friends had been interested in her work for the "pictures" and had kept as closely in touch with her as possible.

It was only when her pictures became generally known and talked about, not only for their absorbing plots but for the powerful bits of drama that made interpretation of the plots unusual, that Ruth felt an irresistible urge to break away from her former affiliations and to undertake the directing of her own pictures, as well as writing the scenarios for them.

The picture *Snowblind* had been the second filmed under her own direction and the amazing and exciting adventures Ruth and her company encountered in the filming of it have been related in the story directly preceding this, entitled "Ruth Fielding in the Far North."

During all Ruth's startling and very successful career, Tom Cameron had been the talented girl's close companion. He had always admired the girl from the Red Mill, even when they were youngsters together; but when Ruth's extraordinary ability developed this admiration changed to worship that had a little of awe in it. Ruth was well aware of Tom's feeling for her and, though she was fond of the young fellow, strove to keep Tom and his emotions as much in the background as possible. Ruth had no intention of marrying and "settling down" until she had proved to her own complete satisfaction just how far she could go in her chosen line of work. While Tom accepted this attitude he was, naturally, a trifle at odds with it.

However, during the preceding year Tom had become Ruth's business partner, taking over the tiresome and innumerable details that must always cling to an enterprise as flourishing and ambitious as the Fielding Film Corporation, thus leaving the creative genius of his partner full liberty to soar, as it were, untrammeled.

While this arrangement did not entirely satisfy Tom, it was at least a business partnership and kept him in close touch with Ruth. Then, too, he had become sincerely and absorbedly interested in the motion picture industry on his own account.

Helen's romance was a more satisfactory one from the general viewpoint. She had allowed Chess Copley's ardor to persuade her into an engagement and the two—who often appeared more like amiable enemies than lovers—were merely waiting for Chess to "make his fortune" in order to celebrate the fulfillment of their romance.

So it was that matters stood between these four young folks on this opening night of *Snowblind* and Ruth's brief address to an admiring public.

Now, as Tom fought his way through the smoke-filled theater, he could think of nothing but how fine Ruth had looked on the stage that night and of how proud he had been just to know her.

Now she was in danger. Suppose he could not reach her? Suppose she should be overcome by smoke?

He paused, staggered, brushed a hand across his eyes in an instinctive effort to clear them of the burning, stinging smoke. No flame—only smoke? Where did it all come from? What unheard-of, mysterious thing had happened, anyway?

He flung himself forward, caught at some one who staggered against him.

"Ruth!"

"Oh, Tom!"

Tom half-carried, half-led her toward a door he had stumbled against in his frantic plungings. He yanked at it, pulled it open, felt a swirling rush of fresh air.

"Safe, Ruth, safe!"

CHAPTER 3

GOOD OLD TIMES

Ruth drew in great lungfuls of the fresh air. Her next thought was for Aunt Alvirah and her school friends. She gave Tom's arm a tug and started around toward the front of the theater.

"If any of them are hurt!" Tom heard her murmur, as he followed.

"Take it easy," warned the young fellow, seeing that the girl was dizzy and weak from her terrible experience. "We will go round to the front of the theater. Probably all our crowd have found their way to the street by this time."

As a matter of fact, when Tom and Ruth reached the street they found that the theater had been practically emptied. Crowds had already gathered curiously about the smoke-ridden place. Cheslow's limited police force was trying noisily and rather ineffectually to keep people back. The local fire engines had also arrived and firemen were taking their lines of hose and chemical fire extinguishers into the theater. Smoke, there seemed to be in plenty but scarcely any flames.

Those who had constituted the audience were breaking up into small, shaken groups, some wending their way homeward, intent upon reaching shelter and safety as soon as possible.

Small children were wailing heart-brokenly, women were half hysterical, the men were white and nervous.

But when Ruth's eager eyes, searching, descried her own party, all together and unharmed, as far as she could see, her relief knew no bounds.

She saw them before they discovered her.

Aunt Alvirah and Uncle Jabez were the center of the crowd of excited and gesticulating young folks. The latter seemed trying to soothe and comfort the little old woman, but Aunt Alvirah's quick, dark eyes darted unceasingly in all directions.

When she discovered Ruth and Tom pushing eagerly through the crowd a loud and tremulous cry broke from her old lips.

"My pretty!" she cried. "My pretty!"

14

The next moment Ruth's arms were about the little old woman in a hug hard enough and wild enough to break every bone in the frail old body. However, it is doubtful if Aunt Alvirah would have cared at the moment how many bones she lost as long as Ruth had been returned to her.

"I must say this is a fine show you staged, Ruth Fielding!" remarked Jennie Marchand, regarding Ruth reproachfully. "Trying to exterminate us all as soon as we arrive in Cheslow!"

Ruth laughed unsteadily.

"It wasn't the most cordial reception in the world," she admitted dryly. "But I didn't have a hand in it, girls, honest!"

"Didn't you, now?" It was Mary Cox who spoke with scathing sarcasm.

"Compared to some of those scenes in your picture, Ruth Fielding," laughed Nettie Parsons, "this fire scene held no thrills at all."

"It held enough for me," sighed Mercy Curtis. "It tore a rent in my dress that will never come right again."

"As long as it didn't tear a rent in you," said Helen gayly, "you needn't complain, my dear."

The young folks watched the firemen come and go. Only one stream was turned on and several chemical extinguishers were brought into play, and that was all.

"More smoke than anything," remarked one of the boys.

"Gee, but what an explosion!" remarked another. "I thought the roof was going off!"

Gradually the excitement died down and the crowd was considerably thinned out.

"And now," suggested Chess, who had been silent much longer than usual—probably due to shock—"what do you all say to some eats? I myself am possessed of a hollow void that will require considerable attention on my part to fill."

"How vulgar!" sniffed Helen. "Girls, don't you envy me?"

"It begins to look," said Jennie Marchand, "as though my wedding present to you would be a large, fat and freshly-edited cook book."

"Jennie," sighed Chess ecstatically, "you certainly are a friend of mine!"

Ruth cut short the interchange of nonsense by suggesting that Aunt Alvirah should be taken somewhere out of the chill of the damp night air. Uncle Jabez, having had enough excitement for one night, announced that he was going home. But Helen would not hear of his returning so soon, knowing that Aunt Alvirah would think it her duty to go back to the Red Mill with him.

Then Ruth was given her second big surprise of the evening.

"We've arranged a real party for you, Ruth Fielding, at the hotel," Mercy Curtis announced gleefully, laughing eyes on Ruth's astonished face. "*You*

15

are to be the guest of honor. Aunt Alvirah is to sit on your right hand and no one is allowed to go home."

"Until the feast is nothing but a sweet memory," finished Jennie with a sigh.

Every one laughed and in the general merriment no one noticed Uncle Jabez' muttered complaints. They hustled him with Aunt Alvirah into Tom's car.

Ruth lingered before the theater with Nettie Parsons and Barclay Clayton, who was acting as her escort for the evening.

"Some films in the storeroom exploded," said Barclay—popularly known as "Bark"—as he followed the direction of Ruth's gaze to the now almost deserted theater. "Some men were talking about it before you and Tom showed up. Not much fire—mostly smoke."

Ruth nodded. Firemen had easily conquered the small blaze resulting from the explosion and were now leaving the deserted building.

"I hope no one was seriously hurt," Nettie said, as the three, responding to urgent calls from the rest of the party, crossed the pavement. "It was certainly a panic for a while."

"It is lucky," said Ruth soberly, "that some one wasn't killed."

When the party reached the Cheslow hotel and were ushered into the private dining room that Ruth's chums had engaged for the evening in honor of the grand occasion, the excitement and the distressing events of the evening were almost forgotten.

Aunt Alvirah forgot all about the ache in her back and bones of which she had complained monotonously for many years. Even Uncle Jabez brightened perceptibly at sight of the good and plentiful food and set to upon the tempting viands with a will.

"Your picture was a wonder, Ruth," Mercy Curtis called across from her side of the table. "From now on it will be my one ambition to take a trip to your north country."

"It must be wonderful to have all those thrilling adventures," sighed The Fox. "For goodness' sake, don't give me any more nuts, Charles," she said to the attentive young man on her right hand. "Before you know it, I shall turn into one!"

"Turn?" queried Jennie, with an insulting emphasis not missed by Miss Cox, who merely made a face at her in reply.

Ruth said suddenly from her place of honor at the head of the long table:

"Girls, this is so exactly like old times that I feel I must be dreaming. You can't any of you be real!"

"Gaze upon the fast-disappearing food, Ruth, and behold the refutation of your dream," chuckled Jennie Marchand. "Phantoms never ate like these. Pass me a pickle some one, ere I starve!"

"Anyway," Ruth persisted, "now that I have you all here in Cheslow, you shan't get away easily! Isn't that so, Aunt Alvirah?"

The latter nodded cordially, though Uncle Jabez was seen to glance up sharply at his niece.

"There isn't anything you want, my pretty, that I don't want, too," said the little old woman simply.

Ruth squeezed her hand beneath the table and said so softly that no one else could hear:

"We will have some one in from the village to help. You shan't have any more work, Auntie."

Helen was speaking, and with an emphasis that caught Ruth's attention.

"If you think you are going to have the girls all to yourself, Ruth Fielding, you never were more mistaken in all the course of your eventful career. I intend to do some entertaining, too!"

Ruth was about to make some laughing reply when the door opened suddenly. Every one turned toward the sound. Ruth gave a little gasp of surprise and delight. She rose quickly and went forward with outstretched hands.

"Mr. Hammond! Well, this is my night of surprises!"

Mr. Hammond was immediately dragged to the table and a waiter was directed to bring another plate for him at once.

"I hoped to reach Cheslow in time for the run-off of your picture," the president of the Alectrion Film Corporation said, his face ruddier and pleasanter than ever. "I wanted particularly to hear your address. But I was detained by business that would not be put off."

"It was good of you to come at all," said Ruth, hospitably making sure that his plate was well filled with good things.

CHAPTER 4

GOLDEN PASS

Mr. Hammond needed no introduction to Aunt Alvirah or Uncle Jabez, since he had known the old couple as long as he had known Ruth herself.

Neither did Ruth's chums need any special introduction since they considered themselves—and with reason—long-standing acquaintances of the head of the Alectrion Film Corporation.

For it was Mr. Hammond who had accepted Ruth's early scenario which she had called "The Heart of a School Girl" and filmed it with the aid of the two hundred odd girls at Briarwood Hall.

Some of the young men he had not met before and these introductions were made hastily and informally. Then Mr. Hammond turned to Ruth.

"I have already heard flattering criticisms of your picture. It will play to full houses for a long time, my dear. I can safely prophesy that."

"Well, I trust they have no more explosions when they show it," answered Ruth with a serious shake of her head.

"That explosion was not so bad as it seemed. Mr. Farstein told me so himself. Merely a lot of discarded films left in the storeroom by one of the distributing firms. More smoke than fire. He is already arranging to clean up the muss so he can open as usual tomorrow. And he said that nobody seemed to be seriously hurt, which is best of all."

"I am awfully glad of that, Mr. Hammond."

"It's the Ruth Fielding luck," and Mr. Hammond smiled. "And now that this picture is a success I suppose you are already figuring on doing something else as big or bigger," he went on.

"I am," Ruth answered quietly.

"Ah, I thought so! The old spirit. More worlds to conquer, aren't there? Where is the new drama of the silver screen to be laid?" the motion picture magnate went on curiously.

"In the most beautiful spot in the world—or so we're told on very good authority, you yourself! Golden Pass, Montana."

As Ruth spoke there was a sudden cessation of careless chatter. The young folks looked at her eagerly, Aunt Alvirah looked anxiously expectant while Uncle Jabez scowled faintly.

"Montana! Whoop—ee!" cried Helen irrepressibly. "A wild-west picture full of thrilling scenes and good looking cowboys. Ain't I glad I came!"

"You seem to be very sure of your welcome in the party," said Chess severely. "How do you know Ruth will want you to go with her?"

"Oh, Ruth always wants me," replied Helen with a flippancy that belied the gravity of her expression. "As a matter of fact, she couldn't get along without me. She told me so herself!"

Chess grinned.

"Far be it from me—"

But at this point Helen put an end to the sentence by severely pinching the arm of its author.

"Oh, do hush! Don't you see I'm trying to hear what Ruth's saying?"

What Ruth was saying appeared to be of intense interest to the others of the party. They listened eagerly as she described the spot where most of the new picture she had in mind would be filmed.

"Golden Pass will be the ideal spot for the filming of my sort of picture. A land of fertile valleys and picturesque mountains—"

"It is pretty," Mr. Hammond agreed. "As you say, I know the place you speak of, Miss Ruth, for I had to pass through Montana not long ago and I stopped off at Golden Pass. I had heard there was to be a big cattle round-up and I wanted to get pictures of it."

Ruth leaned toward him eagerly.

"Is it so rugged and beautiful?"

"It is. It is a land of plains and hills and steep ravines, of sparkling dawns and gorgeous sunsets. The very finest location possible for an outdoor, western picture."

"Dear me, Ruth Fielding," spoke up Ann Hicks wistfully, "you make me homesick for those wide, open ranges. Can't you take me with you? I can bust bronchos with the best of 'em. Don't you need a really talented extra?"

Ruth laughed.

"I wish I could take you all. Oh, girls, wouldn't that be fun?"

Mr. Hammond shortly took his departure, saying that he would like to see Ruth soon and hear something about her new picture.

His desertion seemed to be the signal for the general breaking up of the party. Aunt Alvirah was looking white and tired and Uncle Jabez was beginning to complain of the lateness of the hour.

It was hard to put an end to the fun. Ruth felt she had never before enjoyed herself so much. It was arranged, despite Ruth's protests, that the visitors to Cheslow were to put up at the Cameron's for the remainder of their stay.

"Don't be a goose, Ruthie," Helen whispered when Ruth was about to insist that she must have at least one of the girls with her at the Red Mill. "You will be rushed to death finishing your scenario and arranging all the details of the trip. We have plenty of room and nothing to do but entertain the girls while they stay. Besides, we shall probably be over at the Red Mill almost every day."

"Well, then, I'll have them all at the Red Mill for a night before we start," Ruth declared. "Even you can't stop me doing that much, Helen Cameron!"

All except Mercy Curtis, who lived in Cheslow, escorted Uncle Jabez, Aunt Alvirah and Ruth home first. Standing at the door with the two old people, Ruth answered the farewells of her friends.

"Good-by, all of you! It was a lovely party! Good-by!"

From down the road, as the little fleet of cars moved off, came softly to Ruth!

> *"S.B.—Ah-h-h!*
> *S.B.—Ah-h-h!*
> *Sound our battle-cry*
> *Near and far!*
> *S.B.—All!*
>
> *Briarwood Hall!*
> *Sweetbriars, do or die—*
> *This be our battle-cry—*
> *Briarwood Hall!*
> *That's all!"*

As they turned to enter the house together Ruth gave Aunt Alvirah a particularly hard hug.

"It *is* a good old world, isn't it, Auntie?" she cried.

The old woman peered up in the girl's face, smiled, and nodded sympathetically.

"So it is, my pretty! So it is!"

The next day proved an eventful one for Ruth. Several days before she had wired Layton Boardman, an interesting young westerner who had served an early apprenticeship on a ranch and had later made a reputation for himself in moving pictures, requesting an interview with him at the Red Mill. Ruth felt sure he was just the one to fill the part of hero in her new picture.

Boardman had recently quarreled with Sol Bloomberg, the chief owner of the Palatial Films Corporation with which Boardman had been for some time associated. It was open gossip in moving picture circles that, since this quarrel, Layton Boardman was finding it hard to place himself with any of the other large motion picture concerns.

This might mean, of course, that Boardman had lost his grip, had gone stale, was no longer desirable. But Ruth, who had seen the actor's last picture and been thrilled by the power of his acting and by the real magnetism of his screen personality, preferred not to believe this.

She thought it far more probable that Sol Bloomberg was pulling strings with the deliberate intention of keeping Boardman from obtaining another position until such time as the actor should be starved into accepting a position from the owner of Palatial Films on the latter's own terms.

Ruth had debated with herself at length upon the wisdom of approaching Boardman in her own interests, for, courageous as she was, she feared Sol Bloomberg—and with reason. But at last her business instinct won. Boardman was exactly the type she needed for the rôle of hero; in fact, she had so come to visualize him in that part that her picture seemed utterly without force or power when she disassociated him from it.

So, taking her courage in both hands, she had sent a telegram, requesting an audience. Boardman had replied promptly, accepting.

Ruth had no idea that the actor himself would appear almost on the heels of his telegram, as it were. But then, Ruth had no idea how near to desperation Layton Boardman was!

So it came to pass that on this morning of the day after the excitement at the theater and the party given in her honor, Ruth was surprised when Aunt Alvirah brought in the actor's card.

Ruth was in the room that she used for her study, deep in the revision and embellishing of her new scenario.

She looked vaguely from Aunt Alvirah to the card of Layton Boardman and back again.

"Are you sure Mr. Boardman gave you this?" she asked, her mind still on her work. "Why, Aunt Alvirah, I had no idea he would get here before tomorrow."

"Well, he's here, my pretty, and as likely a young man as I'm like to see anywhere," said Aunt Alvirah with an emphatic bob of her white head. "Right fine lookin' I'd call him. Reminds me of a picture I see once of a football star—from Yale or Princeton I think 'twas—broad-shouldered an' handsome an' sech a smile!"

Ruth laughed.

"Aunt Alvirah, I'm ashamed of you, falling in love with a strange young man. Don't you know it's up to you to set young folks a good example?"

Aunt Alvirah chuckled.

"I ain't worryin' none over you, my pretty," she said. "An' the question now seems to be not what he looks like but shall I let him in?"

"Oh, please do, Aunt Alvirah." Ruth began hurriedly straightening the papers on her desk.

A shadow fell across her work and she looked up to see a towering figure in the doorway. She had known before that Layton Boardman was a big man, but she had never realized just how big he was. His shoulders seemed to block entirely the opening made by the door.

Ruth smiled and extended her hand.

"I am very glad to see you, Mr. Boardman. I imagine you and I will have a great deal to say to each other."

CHAPTER 5

A NEW STAR

Layton Boardman was fine looking, far better looking than he appeared on the screen. He had one of those faces that appeal to the imagination, usually immobile and inscrutable, yet capable of a surprising play of expression when aroused emotionally. He had black hair and dark gray, rather long eyes, deep set in his head and adding to the inscrutable expression of his face when at rest. If it had not been for his flashing and utterly friendly smile one might almost have been afraid of Layton Boardman.

A wonderful face, a splendid personality for the hero of her western drama—a screen strong man who was as strong off the screen as on!

Something surged up in Ruth—exultation at having secured such a prize. Then fear gripped her again. Suppose he should refuse her offer—want more than she was prepared to pay? Well, she would soon put that question to the test.

"It was nice of you to come so quickly. The fact is," she faced him with her frank smile, "I was wondering whether you were free to accept an offer from the Fielding Film Company."

Boardman made a wry grimace.

"I am certainly at liberty," he said grimly. "So much so," with his quick smile, "that I long for bonds again!"

"Then I hope I shall be the one to slip them on." Ruth was again at her ease. Something told her that she and Layton Boardman would get on.

She fingered some of the papers on her desk, looked from them to Boardman.

"I have a new script here and I need just such a man as you to take the lead. I don't mind admitting," she looked across at him with a quizzical smile, "that I had you in mind when I wrote the story."

"That is about the nicest thing I ever had said to me," he told her. "I hope more than I can tell you that I will be able to live up to that compliment."

"You're sure you're perfectly free? No loose strings that might get tangled up in the midst of the story and spoil the whole thing?"

"Not a string!" said Boardman.

"Then listen to me and see if we can come to terms. We haven't any time to lose, for I'm anxious to keep my company together and start for Montana in two weeks at the outside."

There followed a surprisingly short business conference, during which the two young people seemed to find it very easy to agree on everything.

Ruth felt excited and very much pleased with herself. She had done a good morning's work. She had not dreamed she would be able to procure the services of Layton Boardman at so low a price and—this after she had twice glanced up to find his eyes fixed broodingly upon her—he would certainly make a very pleasant addition to the company.

Ruth heard Tom enter unceremoniously, heard his familiar whistle and his affectionate greeting of Aunt Alvirah. She called to him and checked young Boardman when he rose to go.

"I want you to meet my partner, Tom Cameron," she explained. "His signature will be very necessary on the contract."

Tom hesitated in the doorway, taking in the tableau presented. His next emotion was annoyance. It would be enough to annoy any young fellow to find Layton Boardman, good looks and magnetism apparent even to a man, in private conference with the girl he was—well, was fond of.

Ruth caught the expression on Tom's face and tried to keep her vivid face straight as she explained hurriedly.

"Glad to see you, Boardman," Tom said then, extending his hand. Boardman clasped it heartily. "I have an idea I can feel contracts in the air. Ah—" as Ruth thrust into his hands the agreement she and Boardman had drawn up. "Let me see—"

His very palpable hesitation seemed funny to Ruth. Tom always left the signing up of new actors to her judgment. He had often declared that she knew far more than he concerning such things. He had never made a fuss about anything like this. Was he going to start now?

As his hesitation continued Ruth became really uneasy. When he finally, though somewhat reluctantly it seemed, gave his approval, she drew a deep breath of relief.

As soon as the business was over with three signatures signed to the contract and Aunt Alvirah's added as a witness, Layton Boardman took his departure. He had, it seemed, important matters to attend to in town and he left the Red Mill despite Aunt Alvirah's hospitable urging that he stay and have a bite of lunch with them.

Long after the door had closed upon the new member of Ruth's company Tom remained silent and thoughtful. Ruth tried to start a conversation with him, for she was full of excitement and pleasure over what she considered a triumph. But when he failed to respond to her advances she finally retired to her study, leaving Tom to his own devices.

She had scarcely had time to become engrossed in her work again, however, before a shadow fell across her page and she looked up to find Tom glooming in the doorway. Ruth tapped her pencil on the edge of the desk in helpless exasperation.

"What is wrong with you, Tom Cameron?" she cried. "You look as if you had lost your last friend and never expected to make another. What in the world *is* the matter?"

"I don't like that fellow, Boardman," said Tom, frowning. "He's too good looking to be honest."

Ruth gave a gay little laugh.

"Layton Boardman has a reputation for honesty—"

"Oh, I suppose he has all the virtues in the pack!" Tom was almost barking at her in his irritation. "The good looking ones can get away with anything. How about that row he had with Sol Bloomberg?"

A shadow crossed Ruth's face. Sol Bloomberg was the lone fly in the ointment of her content. She had been trying to forget Sol Bloomberg. But now she shrugged her shoulders, trying to make the gesture nonchalant.

"Knowing Sol Bloomberg, I prefer to think the fault was his," she said.

"I think so, too," said Tom with native honesty. "But there are two sides to every question, you know, and there is always the chance that Boardman's side wasn't a pleasant one. Then, too," his gravity deepened, "if there wasn't anything more to it than a question of Bloomberg's enmity, it would be worth considering—and hesitating over. Bloomberg isn't going to be very happy when he learns that we've signed up his star at a good salary."

"His ex-star," Ruth reminded him.

"Ex-star or not, Bloomberg wants Layton Boardman, and if I know anything of the man in question, he'll get Boardman, no matter how many promising young moving picture concerns he has to trample over in the process."

"But do you suppose," Ruth flamed at him, "I intend to let a chance like this slip simply because I'm afraid of Sol Bloomberg?"

"A great many people, both powerful and wise, have been afraid of Sol Bloomberg," retorted Tom and, thrusting his hands deep into his pockets, strode from the room.

Ruth tried in vain to coax back her mood of the early morning. But try as she would, it would not come. Tom had effectually destroyed all her enthusiasm with his talk of Sol Bloomberg. The worst of it was, Ruth admitted, that his viewpoint was a reasonable one. The owner of Palatial Films would be furious over her capture of Boardman, and Bloomberg was not a man to swallow his anger.

With an impatient movement she began to gather up her scattered papers when Helen Cameron and Jennie Marchand, arms about each other in old-time style, charged in at the front door.

"Ruthie! Ruthie Fielding, where are you?" called Helen. "I have the very most elegant news you ever listened to! Let me tell it, else I die!"

CHAPTER 6

FINE NEWS

The arrival of Helen and Jennie Marchand was like a breath of fresh air, blowing away the cobwebs in Ruth's worried mind.

Helen explained that the other girls had gone motoring with their friends of the evening before and had sent word to Ruth that they would probably stop in at the Red Mill later in the day.

Jennie was puffing with hard exercise and blamed Helen for making her walk so fast.

"Now that I am a young matron and not a harum-scarum schoolgirl," she said, as primly as Jennie could, "I prefer to walk rather than run to my appointments."

"Cheer up, you're not the only pebble on the beach," Helen retorted flippantly, as she flung herself into a corner of the old couch. "Before long I myself may become that awfully uninteresting, fearfully settled, dried up old prune that people kindly term a young matron!"

Jennie giggled, but Ruth glanced at her friend quickly. She could see that beneath Helen's flippant manner was an undercurrent of excitement, of pleasure. Something important had happened to Helen.

She went over and perched on the arm of her chum's chair.

"Helen," she said, "you may pull the wool over the eyes of most people, but you'd better not try it with your Ruth. It won't work."

"You precious old thing!" Helen reached up and stroked Ruth's hand fondly. "I wouldn't try to pull anything over those perfectly gorgeous orbs of yours, Ruthie. It would be a sin and a shame."

"Then what," persisted Ruth, "was that news you were threatening to die of when you burst in the door?"

"I didn't burst in," Helen protested, but was rudely shaken by her friend.

"Out with it, or you shan't come to Montana with me!"

"Oh, what a threat! You could never do such a thing to me, Ruth. You have too big a heart. Oh, that reminds me, you were waiting to hear about my news."

"We're waiting," agreed Jennie dryly.

27

"Well, it isn't so much, really, except as it affects me—and Chess," Helen began, and Ruth could tell by the restraint in her voice that Helen's news was of an emotional nature. It was always hard for Helen to maintain her gravity in moments of sentiment. She hesitated for a moment, then said, quite suddenly, glancing up at Ruth: "You remember that uncle of Chess's who owned what you called the 'snowball property' up North?"

Ruth's eyes danced. She was intensely interested.

"Quite vividly," she nodded. "Also I remember the day we went with Delabarre and Briais, all comfy and snug in the sled behind the dog team to look the property over."

"And the time shortly after that," Helen added, squeezing her chum's hand in the painful memories revived by the recollection, "when you jumped into the pit with half a dozen bears and did your best to get yourself eaten up by them."

"There were only three bears," Ruth corrected demurely.

"Oh, dear," sighed Heavy, from her place as onlooker to all these wonderful adventures, "you girls have all the fun while I have to stay at home and take care of Henri."

"Probably that is quite as exciting at times as falling into a pit with three wild animals," said Helen gravely.

"Married life at times," chuckled Jennie, "would certainly make such an adventure look tame!"

"Is that why you've left home now, Heavy, and left your Henri in France?" asked Helen.

And then they laughed happily at such absurdity and Ruth urged Helen again to go on with her story.

"What about the uncle and the 'snowball property'?" she prompted.

"This darling precious old uncle," Helen replied, "is willing to back Chess in a big business deal that has been hanging fire for some time on account of a small and inconsiderable thing such as the lack of ready cash. Chess's uncle is willing to supply the cash, which seems to make everything lovely."

Ruth's arm tightened about her chum's shoulder. She had read more into the laughing sentence than Helen had said in words.

"And that means—" she prompted.

"Oh, Ruthie, it means," Helen's voice sank so low that Ruth had to bend over her to hear at all, "that Chess and I won't have to go on waiting any more. Money seems to clear the way for most everything, doesn't it? Of course, we wouldn't have starved, but Chess wanted to stand on his own feet. And I just love him for that!"

"Well, just listen to my kid sister! She's actually getting sentimental!"

The girls looked up, startled, to see Tom grinning at them from the doorway.

Before they could think of anything to say he advanced into the room and stood, hands in pockets, staring down thoughtfully at the discomfited Helen.

"I suppose," he said with tremendous gravity, "it's up to me to kiss the bride!"

"If you dare!" cried his ungrateful sister. She seized a pillow and poised it threateningly. "Get out of here, Tommy. Didn't you know I was speaking to my friends?"

"Oof!" grunted Tom, as he chose discretion and promptly retreated. "I'm not a friend. I'm only a brother!"

They laughed a little, and Ruth and Jennie questioned Helen eagerly after the manner of most girls on such occasions.

At the end Ruth put her arm about her chum and said softly:

"I'm glad for you and Chess, my dear. You and Chess will be mighty happy."

"Poor old 'Lasses," sighed Jennie. "As my great aunt said to her son's fiancée on the eve of the young couple's marriage, 'Poor dear Harry, he was such a happy boy!'"

It was then that Jennie received the full impact of the sofa cushion which, but a moment before, had threatened Tom.

Ruth laughed.

"Don't let Heavy fuss you, Helen," she said. "Harry may have been a happy boy and a still happier man."

"But we know Helen!" interposed Jennie.

"Just so!" retorted Ruth. "Chess's chances for bliss are excellent."

"Thank you, Ruthie, for them kind words," murmured Helen, her eyes dancing.

Jennie and Helen stayed to lunch and went for a walk soon afterward, leaving Ruth once more to the task of revising and perfecting her scenario.

She found it unusually hard to concentrate on her work. There was still the fear that she had made a mistake in engaging Boardman.

Tom found her bent over the manuscript, brow furrowed, looking tired and harassed.

"You have done enough work for today, Ruth Fielding," he told her. Before she could prevent him he had gathered up the pages of her manuscript and put them away definitely in a drawer. She made a motion as though to open the drawer, whereupon Tom calmly locked it and pocketed the key.

"Now what are you going to do about it?" he challenged, grinning at her.

"But, Tom, I haven't done a speck of real work today," she protested. "And there is so much to do!"

"Not all at once," said Tom. "The whole trouble with Ruth Fielding is that she never knows when to stop working."

"I certainly am glad you know what's wrong with her," said Ruth, with a doleful sigh. "I've been trying all day to find out."

Tom laughed cheerfully, got to his feet, seized Ruth's hands and pulled her up beside him.

"Come on! What you need is a breath of fresh air. You've no idea how good fresh air is for ideas," he added gravely as Ruth, protesting, allowed herself to be led outside to Tom's car which stood waiting for them. "It seems just to breed 'em!"

Ruth laughed helplessly.

"I have an idea right now that I am being kidnapped against my better judgment," she said.

"You know better!" Tom grinned at her as he slid in behind the low-slung wheel. "You were just pining for some nice strong man to come along and separate you from your arduous labors. Besides," he added with a long and doleful sigh, "I feel that it is up to me to make hay while the sun shines."

Ruth looked at him curiously. The wind on her face did feel good. All her worries seemed to have vanished in the swift rush of it.

"Just what did you mean by that?" she queried.

Tom looked at her quizzically.

"With that handsome Boardman chap on the premises, I can see where old Tom will have to watch his step!"

Ruth laughed contentedly.

"You old silly! How lucky you would be, Tommy boy, if you never had anything worse than that to worry about."

CHAPTER 7

THE LEADING LADY

The days that followed were busy and pleasant ones for Ruth. Even when her doubt concerning the wisdom of engaging Layton Boardman and thus inviting Sol Bloomberg's enmity would crop up, she put it resolutely from her. She certainly did not intend to borrow trouble.

Then, too, she thought often of Tom's laughing remark concerning the attractive western actor. Could it be that Tom was really inclined to be jealous of this man, whom, so far, she hardly knew? The idea was too absurd to be seriously considered.

Helen and Chess were openly happy over the good fortune of the latter. The big business deal which had been hanging fire for some time held almost the certainty of success, now that Chess had secured the necessary amount of credit to push it through.

No wonder they were happy! Their happiness was contagious, which was one reason, perhaps, that Ruth found herself in such high spirits during that time.

The local paper came out with an account of the fire and of the part Ruth and the others had played in it. The fire had really been a small affair and the theater was once more running as usual, the new film drawing crowded houses.

But *Snowblind* was being shown elsewhere, too—six sets of films of the picture had been made—and Ruth was eager to see what critics in other cities would have to say about it. As the city newspapers came in she read the notices eagerly, as did Tom.

"A knockout, Ruth!" cried the young man. "A regular knockout everywhere!" And he was right, in every city where it was shown *Snowblind* was a big success.

Ruth's chums still stayed on in Cheslow. They visited the Red Mill almost every day, occasionally staying to dinner or some other meal, and they never failed to declare that they were having the "time of their lives."

They were receiving a good deal of attention from the young men of Cheslow, and, since most of these were well-off and owned their own cars,

31

the girls naturally did not lack for pleasant occupation. Jennie, as chaperone, was enjoying herself hugely. It was not in Jennie to be formal, still in France, as Madame Marchand, she put some restraint on herself, which now in the midst of her old school friends she threw off entirely and became once more the old "Heavy" Stone of their Briarwood days.

Ruth was, of course, invited to attend all these parties, and at first her old friends seemed a bit offended when she refused, pleading her work.

However, it was not long before, with Helen's loyal assistance, they were able to understand that Ruth's work did make heavy demands on her time and was not a light pastime to be attended to in odd moments.

If it had not been such a particularly busy time with Ruth she would have liked nothing better than to have joined in all the fun with her friends. As it was, she was able to accompany them once in a while, and she never failed to return from one of the merrymakings strengthened in mind and with a fund of fresh enthusiasm for her work.

Meanwhile plans for the house party which she meant to give her old school chums before the end of their visit were taking definite shape.

Although the accommodations of the house at the Red Mill were limited she could manage to put the girls up for a night; at least, all except Mercy, who lived in Cheslow, and Helen, who would go back with Tom and the other young fellows whom Ruth had already invited to the party.

Ruth had made inquiries in Cheslow and found that she could secure the services of a young girl to help Aunt Alvirah with the work.

It would be a lark, and Ruth was looking forward to it eagerly.

Meanwhile, there was a great deal of work to be done. Ruth was anxious to finish all details connected with her new picture so that they might start for Montana as soon as possible.

The script was finished. She had gone over it with Tom and, still later, with Layton Boardman.

Both young men were pleasantly enthusiastic. The actor had offered suggestions here and there that, Ruth felt, strengthened the script.

She liked Layton Boardman's free and easy western manner that was yet always pleasant and respectful to her. And she liked the way he took hold of the part she offered him. She became more and more convinced that she had found the right actor for her drama.

Another thing that engaged her attention was the problem of the feminine lead. She could not use Anita Townsend, the star of "Snowblind." It was not the rôle suited to Anita. She must have an actress for the lead in "Hearts of the Mountains," and that quickly.

She and Tom had discussed most of the stars on the horizon and found the majority of them—at least those fitted for the part—tied up already by handsome contracts.

"Viola Callahan is the ideal one for our purpose," said Ruth, in one of her many conferences with Tom. "And I think her five-year contract with Brennan has about run out. Still——"

"Try her and see," suggested Tom. "The most she can do is refuse."

But Viola did not refuse. Like the majority of shining stars in Filmdom, she had chosen to exercise her temperament, and in a fit of rage had thrown her contract—literally—in the face of an outraged manager. Since this contract was nearly expired, having only three weeks to run, and since the fair Viola had allowed her temper to run away with her several times during the past five years with disastrous results to the company in general, Mr. Brennan had decided—with a sigh of relief—to let his western beauty go.

Now, it is one thing to throw your contract away and quite another to have it politely handed back to you with the request that you keep it and do with it what you please. The pride of a genius would not allow Viola to humble herself to the point of asking the polite Mr. Brennan for a chance to go on again, so she found herself, for the first time in many years, without a sign of a job.

Viola did not fancy this very much, and was in a state of mind to receive Ruth's overtures graciously.

So it came to pass that not long after her conversation with Tom, Ruth found herself in audience with the fair Viola herself.

Viola seemed out of place, someway, in the quaint, old-fashioned living room of the Red Mill. She was flamboyant in dress and action and so overflowing with vitality that one felt her presence in a room even before she began to speak. And then, to use Ruth's own phrase, "one was simply overwhelmed with Viola."

The girl had beauty after a fashion, although the screen did something to her features, softened them, refined them, made them infinitely more appealing than they appeared in the full and brutal light of day.

But Ruth had seen the girl on the screen many times, knew that she could act, and in her picture would be an effective opposite to Layton Boardman.

Viola rather took her breath away on the subject of salary. However, after considerable hesitation, Ruth signed her up at a figure which she knew was going to cause considerable worry in the weeks to come. With Viola's salary to be paid every week, there would be little allowance for delay or drawback of any kind. And in the making of a picture, delays and drawbacks are the rule.

After the business part of the interview was at an end, Viola chose to become expansive, taking Ruth into her confidence almost, as Ruth said afterward to Tom, as though Ruth were an old friend.

"You've got a nice place here," she said, wandering about the room, touching small ornaments here and there. "Old-fashioned and homey with plenty of windows and sun coming in at them. The kind of place me and Tony was to have sometime." She heaved a huge sigh and Ruth looked at her curiously.

"Tony?" she repeated. "Do you mean Tony Martano?"

Tony Martano was a name well known in the picture world, though the man himself had never risen beyond the rank of second-rate player.

Viola stopped roaming about the room and sat down in a big chair close to Ruth's, assuming a languid posture. She seemed willing, almost eager, to talk of her blighted romance.

"You know how handsome Tony is," she said. "Well, I guess it was his looks that got me, for there's nothing inside here," she tapped her forehead significantly, "but a solid mass of bone."

Ruth laughed.

"I always thought he was a pretty good actor," she said.

"What he got, his looks got for him," Viola said with brutal frankness. "If he'd had an ounce of brains he'd have edged some other leading man off the map long before this. It only goes to show," with another tremendous sigh, "that love is a funny thing."

"Then you love him still?" asked Ruth. She was rather taken aback by this frankness on the part of Viola, especially to one who but a few moments before had been a total stranger. However, she supposed a great many things could be laid to that mysterious thing called temperament. Something told her that Viola was full of temperament!

"Love him!" cried Viola, rolling her large and rather prominent black eyes. "What I wouldn't do for that man! And do you know," she leaned forward and fixed Ruth with a tragic gaze, "the only thing that stands between us and a little nest of our own?"

"What?" asked Ruth, with difficulty keeping herself from smiling.

"Jealousy!" hissed Viola, and settled back with a satisfied compression of her overfull lips.

"What kind of jealousy?" asked Ruth, bewildered. "Yours or his, professional or personal?"

"His!" snapped Viola, evidently put out that this could be misunderstood even for a moment. "And it's entirely professional. That's what proves him a bonehead. No one should ever let anything stand in the way of love—do you think so?" Viola had become languorous again and Ruth stirred restlessly beneath her look. She wished suddenly that the girl would go. There were so many things to do!

"No," she said in answer to a repeated question from her guest, "I don't suppose anything ought to stand in the way of love—if it's the right kind."

She thought of these words after Viola had gone and smiled a bit ruefully herself.

"I wonder if I meant that? At any rate I don't practice what I preach," she told herself. And still later, in reviewing that interview with Viola, she added: "I don't like that girl. For some reason I distrust her, though I can't for the life of me tell why!"

CHAPTER 8

THE PARTY

The next day Ruth had her first business quarrel with Tom. It was over the salary she had agreed to pay Viola Callahan.

"She isn't worth it," he protested doggedly.

"It isn't any more than she's been getting right along with Brennan," came from Ruth.

"Well, you notice Brennan wasn't so anxious to get her back when she jumped her contract."

"No wonder. Neither would I."

"Yes, you would," Tom persisted. "That is, you would if she were a good enough actress."

"She is a good actress."

"Not good enough for that salary."

"Tom, please don't let's discuss it any more. Maybe I did do wrong—although I don't think so. Only time will prove that. And in the meantime, we're wasting time sitting here and arguing about it. You wanted Viola, yourself, you know you did. And I'm sure she'll carry the lead nicely and if she does and makes this picture the success I'm hoping for it, we could afford to pay her a much larger salary."

"Yes, I know we could," Tom capitulated at last. "And we won't say anything more about it, Ruth, since it's done, though I undoubtedly have a right to be consulted beforehand on money matters. But our job now is to pitch into the making of pictures and make this one the finest yet. Certainly no amount of Viola Callahans could spoil that."

He said nothing further, but Ruth had an uneasy feeling that Tom's mind was not changed in the least. And this attitude of his seemed only to add to her responsibility. If everything went well—very well! If not—

The night of the party arrived at last.

Ruth was in wonderful spirits. This was due partly to anticipation of the party, partly to the fact that she and Tom and Helen could expect to start for Chicago in a few days' time and from there to Montana.

Mercy Curtis was obliged to decline Ruth's invitation. The girls were to come over from Helen's in the afternoon, bag and baggage. Though Jennie Marchand declared she had only brought a "toothbrush and nightie" with her, it was noticed that her bag was the biggest and heaviest of all.

This was Wednesday. The big party was for that night, and the next day the girls were all to start back home.

"We've stayed so long now," said Ann Hicks. "It's a wonder our families don't disown us!"

Jennie, she thought, would probably stay on for a few days longer, accompanying Ruth and Helen and Tom when they started for Chicago.

It happened that Layton Boardman came down to the Red Mill that afternoon to see Ruth on a matter of business, knowing nothing of the party. Aunt Alvirah, who had been immensely taken with the cowboy actor from the start, insisted that he stay to dinner and the party afterward.

Ruth could do nothing but second the old lady's invitation, though she knew Uncle Jabez would growl at the necessity of entertaining an actor in his house. Then, too, she was not at all sure that the other members of the party would enjoy having Boardman thrust upon them.

However, she need not have worried. Layton Boardman proved even more friendly and pleasant than Ruth had thought him. In the quiet dignity of the old house there was little of the wild open plains suggested in his manner or bearing. He was unaffected and at home, and it was not long before the delighted girls and boys discovered that he possessed a quiet wit that was convulsing.

"I love your hero, Ruth," Nettie Parsons confessed before the evening was half over.

And a little later came in a whisper from Helen:

"If I weren't so terribly in love with Chess, Ruthie—you needn't smile, you bad thing—I think my heart would be in several little pieces by this time. Ruthie, you're in danger. Our handsome hero admires you immensely!"

Nonsense, of course; but pleasant nonsense. Ruth's contentment grew as she realized what a splendid time every one was having.

They pushed back the furniture and danced. There also Layton Boardman shone and Ruth thought that if his skill on horseback was nearly as finished as his skill in dancing it must be very great indeed.

The actor danced with all the girls in turn, a fact which Ruth knew they would never stop talking about when they returned home. But the girl of the Red Mill was amused to find that after Boardman had danced with her twice in succession Tom took possession of her and denied all further requests on the part of the actor.

"Didn't I tell you I was going to watch my step when that fellow was around?" said Tom in answer to the amused twinkle in her eye.

"Well, see that you do!" Ruth admonished severely. "You stepped on my toe that time, Tommy. My best satin slippers, at that!"

Long before refreshments were served Uncle Jabez went to bed. His action was patently intended to express his disapproval of the "goings on."

Aunt Alvirah, however, stayed up to the last moment, sitting in a corner of the room, her old face wreathed in smiles and her old back upright, despite the stiffness of it.

It was long past midnight before the party broke up and then, as the girls said, they had fairly "to push the boys out the front door."

"It's lucky," sighed Jennie as the automobiles tooted off down the road bearing Layton Boardman along with them, "that the girls are going home tomorrow, Ruth Fielding. That hero of yours is far too good looking to be allowed around loose."

"He isn't," said Ruth, stretching luxuriously. "I have him all sewed up with a nice contract. But, oh, the money the Fielding Film Company has to pay that man!"

The next day Ann Hicks went to visit her aunts and Nettie Parsons and Mary Cox went home. Jennie Marchand was to spend a few days more with Helen before going back to New York, to resume her interrupted visit there.

Tom took them to the station, Helen and Ruth and Jennie going along to say good-bye. Several others—of the male population of Cheslow—were gathered on the platform for the same purpose. Consequently the girls were given a rousing good send off.

"The next time we come, Ruth Fielding," said Mary Cox, poking her head out the window as the train began to move, "we will come prepared to stay at least a year!"

"It was like old times, having them," murmured Ruth. "I wish they might have stayed a year! And now," turning with an eager smile to Tom, "for Montana—and adventure."

"There ought to be plenty of that," Tom agreed.

CHAPTER 9

ON THE ROAD

The day dawned gloriously bright, a sparkling day of sunshine and fresh sweet winds and the scent of adventure in the air. It was *the* day on which the start for Montana was to be made.

Ruth never failed to start on a trip of this kind without a thrill of the sort that had come to her on that eventful day of her childhood when she and Helen Cameron had set out for Briarwood Hall.

Adventure was before her. She was happy, exhilarated, free as the air that blew in at her window. Helen and Jennie Marchand had spent the night with Ruth at the Red Mill. This was a precaution taken by Ruth so that they might start early enough to catch the train. Ruth had made arrangements for her company to meet in Chicago, though Viola Callahan and Boardman were to travel with her own party, boarding the train, however, before it reached Cheslow, and Ruth had no intention of missing the train.

Now, in the mirror, she caught Helen's eye, saw that it was fixed mischievously upon her.

"I am wondering," Helen explained in reply to Ruth's raised eyebrows, "how long you are going to go without bobbing your hair."

"I notice you don't bob yours," Ruth retorted, doing up her mane of hair.

Helen grimaced and searched for a shoe under the bed.

"Chess doesn't like it, that's the only reason."

Ruth chuckled.

"I thought you were an emancipated, modern girl," she gibed. "But already you're letting Chess tell you what to do."

"Well, no one can accuse you of that fault as far as Tom is concerned," Helen retorted. Then after a minute, as Ruth did not reply, she said: "Tom is miffed over your handsome actor, Ruth."

"So much the worse for Tom, my dear," Ruth retorted brightly. "And if you think you're going to spoil this beautiful day for me, you're mistaken. Hurry and get dressed, old slow-poke, or we may go without you, after all."

They made a merry breakfast of it, despite the fact that Aunt Alvirah was tearful at the thought of parting again with "her pretty" and that Uncle

Jabez was frankly disapproving of this "gallivantin' off to the ends of the earth for the takin' of ornery pitchers."

By this time, however, Uncle Jabez' scolding was mere habit. He by no means objected to the returns on some money he had put into one of Ruth's pictures.

Tom and Chess came over in time for the early breakfast, parked their cars outside, and declared that everything was ready for the start.

Chess noticed Aunt Alvirah's depression and immediately commenced to sympathize with her.

"Cheer up, Aunt Alvirah," Chess said, patting the old woman on the back. "If you don't stop crying I'll have to start, too, out of sympathy, and I don't want Helen to carry away such a picture of me. She might marry one of those handsome cowboys in the West and never come back. You and I are in the same boat, Auntie, except that Ruth is leaving you on business and Helen hasn't even that excuse."

"He'll make me cry in a minute," said Ruth, with a chuckle. "Poor, neglected chap!"

"You know very well you told me you'd have to be away on business," Helen reminded her fiancé. "I didn't know you would be so broken-hearted at my desertion or I might have changed my mind," she added.

"Please don't," said Ruth. "You must go along, Helen! I couldn't do without you!"

"Hear that?" said Helen, with a triumphant glance at her grinning fiancé. "I told you so!"

It was Uncle Jabez who reminded them that they had better not spend all morning at breakfast if they expected to catch their train.

"I don't believe Uncle Jabez altogether approves of your trip," said Helen as she and Ruth went upstairs to get their wraps on.

Ruth smiled.

"Poor old dear, my aspirations have been a tremendous trial to him. He complains that he's too old to change his ideas at his time of life. But it's not as bad as he lets on."

The good-bye was harder than Ruth had anticipated. Aunt Alvirah clung to her, and, as Ruth had a vision of the lonely days the old woman would spend waiting for her return, some of her own high enthusiasm fled.

"I'd like to tie you up in a big bundle and take you along with me, Auntie," she said, holding the frail old woman close.

"I wish you could, my pretty. I wish you could," sighed Aunt Alvirah, bravely blinking back the tears and giving Ruth a little push toward the others, waiting in Tom's car. "And now you'd better run along, honey, or you'll miss your train for sure. Say good-bye to your Uncle Jabez. He'll be lonesome too."

Though Ruth knew the old man was really sorry to see her go, he hid all emotion carefully, merely expressing a hope that she'd behave herself and come back before they all "was dead and buried."

The tooting of Tom's horn called Ruth away, though she stole one last hug from Aunt Alvirah. Tom opened the door of the car for her and as Ruth stumbled into the seat beside him reached out a hand to steady her.

Ruth waved her hand as the car started down the drive, found the vision of the old lady blurred by tears, then turned to Tom as he sat behind the wheel, watchful eyes on the road ahead.

They reached the station and found they had reached it none too soon, for as the car slid up on one side of the station the train slid to a stop on the other.

Chess had volunteered to take Tom's car back for him and see it safely in the garage.

Tom herded them all into the train, including Jennie Marchand who had determined to accompany the party part way and make another visit before returning to her father's home in New York.

They found their car easily enough and Chess went aboard with them to see that everything was all right and that Helen was comfortably settled for the trip. Here they found Viola and Boardman in their seats.

Chess Copley got off at the last possible minute and stood on the platform waving to Helen. Then it was over and they were on their way to Chicago. A rather queerly assorted party, at that, and one that was sure to attract attention on the train.

Layton Boardman's photographs were so well known that a low, excited whisper and a curious craning of necks followed him wherever he went.

Viola was recognized also, though not so generally. It was not long before all the members of the party were known, and their mission too, in a vague way, by practically every person on the train.

Each time she went into the dining car Ruth felt as though the eyes of every one were upon her. So she would not be at all sorry when they should enter upon the last stage of the trip.

They dropped Jennie Marchand at her destination, but not before they had promised the young matron on their honor to write her "books" concerning their adventures in Montana.

They were all sorry to see Jennie go. If it had not been for Henri Marchand—a rather important obstacle—and her other friends whom Jennie wished to see while on this American visit, they would have taken "Heavy" along with them for the whole time.

"But Henri says I may have just two months in America and must then come back to France and to him," insisted Jennie, and her friends had to be content.

They were to arrive at Chicago in an hour, Ruth realized. There they would meet the rest of Ruth's company and start on the real part of the journey—their ultimate destination, Golden Pass, Montana.

There was the inevitable bustle and flurry of donning wraps. The porter gathered their suitcases and other luggage together, to be distributed to their lawful owners on the platform.

Once arrived at Chicago and part of the hurrying throng in the great station, Tom took charge of the party. Ruth always liked to see him do this. He was so quiet yet masterful in his management of people and things.

He hired taxicabs for them all, saw Viola and Boardman into one, handed Ruth and Helen and then followed, himself, into another.

"Phew!" he whistled when the door was slammed shut and they were at last alone. "I feel as if I'd been part of a circus for the past little while. It's good to have the door shut on the stares of the curious."

Helen giggled.

"Viola was the circus. I think she's loads of fun. Why," she shot a curious look from her brother to Ruth, "do you two distrust her so?"

"I don't exactly distrust her," Ruth returned slowly. "I merely have a feeling that you never can tell just what the girl is going to do next."

"Don't think you'll have to worry about Viola," said Tom. "She's only a silly kid. It's Boardman we ought to keep our eyes on."

Ruth flushed. More than once Tom had made her feel that her judgment was not altogether to be relied upon. Very well! Her eyes flashed and she drew a long breath. She'd show him yet!

They drew up before the hotel where Tom had already engaged rooms by wire for themselves as well as the company. A porter came forward to open the door, another crowded close to pick up the luggage.

As Ruth stepped to the sidewalk she glanced about her with dancing eyes. She slipped her arm through Helen's and squeezed it.

"Adventure's in the air. Can you smell it?" she cried gaily. "And this is our starting point!"

CHAPTER 10

A SUSPICIOUS MOVE

The rest of the company were waiting for Ruth and the Camerons and the two stars, in accordance with the agreement. Ruth received them in her sitting room that evening, gave to each one a copy of the new script and requested that all read it thoroughly before they arrived at Montana.

"It will save time for rehearsals," she told them, smiling. "And I have an idea that when we reach Golden Pass we shall want to start shooting scenes fast and furious. Now, let's see! Are we all here?"

She counted them and found them all on hand from Dave Sentner, the comedian of the pictures, who was really the soberest and quietest of men, to the old character man who was to play the part of the aged, deaf trapper in her picture and who was as talkative and as quick-eared as anybody.

There were two cameramen and two assistant directors, experienced and capable men, all. They were glad to see Ruth and eager to start for the scene of the new picture.

Ruth sketched out briefly her scenario for them, pointing out what part theirs would be in the filming and directing of it. While she was speaking the other members of her company gathered around her, listening with interest and now and then nodding approbation.

"Sounds great to me," said Shepley, the tall, thin director who was really Ruth's right hand man, her help and guide in many details of picture making. "Gives a chance for fine scenes and powerful acting."

"The landslide now," said one of the cameramen, eyes gleaming with anticipation. "Zowie, that ought to be a knockout!"

The general enthusiasm of her company would have delighted Ruth more if she had not been so persistently troubled by the subject of the large payroll. Her company numbered a round twenty in all just as they stood in the sitting room of the Chicago hotel. And there would be more when they reached Montana, extras to be picked up on the spot for the purpose of providing local color. But even the humblest extra must be paid.

Ruth sighed, but, seeing that Tom was regarding her questioningly, changed the sigh to a smile. There was no use in borrowing trouble and, for tonight at least, they might be gay!

Having rounded up all her company there was little left to do save to book reservations to Montana. This was Tom's task, and he went out to attend to it, leaving Helen and Ruth alone for the first time since they had left Cheslow.

"I declare, I'd like to have something to eat here, if it was only a chicken sandwich and a glass of milk," said Helen, looking around the cozy sitting room of Ruth's suite. "It's going to take just about all the courage I possess to get all dressed up and face that mob in the dining room."

Ruth laughed.

"I don't see why we can't eat here if we want to," she agreed. "It would be rather nice—and I have one or two changes I ought to make in the script."

She picked up the telephone and called the dining room, giving an order for dinner to be served promptly at seven o'clock.

"I suppose Tommy's invited?" suggested Helen, and Ruth looked at her, flushing a little.

"Tom—of course!" she said briefly, and went back to her work.

There was a long silence while Helen idly turned the pages of a magazine, watching Ruth while she pretended not to do so.

Then, casually, as though the subject had just occurred to her, she said:

"About this awfully good-looking fellow, Boardman, Ruth. You don't share Tom's suspicions of him, do you?"

Ruth deliberately finished the changes she was making in the script, then gathered her papers together and put them away.

"I haven't the slightest reason to suspect Layton Boardman," she said, meeting Helen's glance calmly. "And I'm quite sure Tom hasn't either. Has he been saying things to you about him?"

"Not especially," Helen admitted. "Only hinted that there might be trouble from Sol Bloomberg—a sort of battle for possession, as it were."

"There is a chance we may have trouble with Bloomberg," Ruth returned, the shadow of worry again crossing her face. "But whatever trouble we have I'm quite sure won't come from Layton Boardman."

Helen opened her mouth as though to speak, thought better of it, and closed it again.

Ruth skillfully turned the subject to lighter things and no more was said concerning Bloomberg that evening. Dinner was served promptly at seven and Tom returned in plenty of time for his share of it.

"Now, children," said Helen, as Tom entered the door of the apartment followed immediately by the waiter bearing the dinner, "I refuse to allow you to talk shop this evening. You may talk sense or nonsense and we will eat. But no moving pictures shall be mixed with the dinner."

44

"Aren't you going to let Tom report as to the time of leaving?" asked Ruth.

"No, not before eating. Um-um!" she went on. "Chicken-a-la-king! The crispest of lettuce! And these rolls—"

"Merely chicken hash, if you ask me," put in Tom.

"Come, Tommy-boy, cheer up," observed his twin.

Tom did cheer up, and the meal went on merrily, all worry, all thoughts of business, pushed into the background.

"It *is* a comfort to get away from that mob downstairs," remarked Tom, as he threw himself into an easy chair to sip his after-dinner coffee.

"Yes," agreed Ruth. "Still, I do love the work and the excitement of it all. But now, Tom, what were the fortunes of the afternoon?" But with her question all her cheerfulness left her, and once more a look of worry came into her eyes.

Tom declared that fortune had been with him and that he had been able to secure reservations for the entire company on the train leaving Chicago for Montana at ten o'clock the following morning.

Her enthusiasm once more alight at the prospect of starting so soon, Ruth forgot about Sol Bloomberg and the possibility of trouble from that quarter.

She was forcibly reminded of it, however, the following morning and in a way which she could least have expected.

She and Helen had run out early to do a bit of shopping before the train started—Helen simply had to have a new hat!—when they met Viola Callahan. The latter was evidently bound on the same mission as themselves and offered to take them around to her favorite hat shop.

Always willing to be shown where millinery was concerned, the two girls accompanied her readily enough. What struck them as suspicious was the abrupt manner in which the girl took her departure after introducing them to the shop. Uttering something entirely unintelligible, she suddenly darted off into the crowd, leaving Ruth and Helen to stare after her, amazed and questioning.

"I bet she saw some one she wanted to talk to in a hurry," said Helen excitedly. "Come on, Ruthie, let's see for ourselves."

Ruth allowed herself to be hurried along through the crowd. Several times they thought they had missed Viola entirely and were tempted to give up the absurd chase.

Then Ruth suddenly caught Helen's arm and drew her to a standstill.

"Over there!" she whispered. "Near the corner! And she's talking to— oh, Helen—it can't be!"

But it was! Ruth's second glance told her that beyond all shadow of a doubt the man with whom Viola Callahan was engaged in earnest conversation was none other than an agent of Sol Bloomberg's.

Ruth knew the man only slightly, but she was well aware that his reputation for shady dealing and shrewd ruthlessness was only second to that of his employer. A worthy servant of a worthy master.

"Who is it? Who is that man talking to Viola?" Helen was whispering excitedly at her elbow.

"Sh-h! Don't let them see we've caught them." Ruth grasped Helen's hand excitedly. "Let's get out of this!"

It was not until their faces were once more turned toward the hotel, their search for a hat temporarily forgotten, that Ruth would explain the curious incident.

"It probably doesn't mean a thing," she said then, trying to speak naturally. "But that man is an agent for Sol Bloomberg. I know him slightly and his reputation much better," she added grimly.

Helen thought this over for a moment.

"What do you gather from it?" she asked.

"Nothing in particular," Ruth answered slowly. "As I said, I may be borrowing trouble. Viola may have met Charlie Reid by accident. It may have been simply a chance encounter. Then again——"

"She may have met him by appointment! It seemed curious the way she left us and dashed off into the crowd——"

"As though she wanted to get rid of us and was rather afraid she might be followed," Ruth finished, meeting her chum's excited gaze. "Yes, it does seem strange. And then, her talking to that man at this time——"

"What do you think he—or rather, Sol Bloomberg—wants of her?" asked Helen, her mind turning over this new development. She loved intrigue of any kind. "Do you think he wants to sign her up for himself?"

"Stranger things have happened," Ruth answered dryly.

"But she has a contract with you," said Helen. "Duly signed and witnessed."

"Actresses," Ruth returned in the same tone, "have been known to jump their contracts."

"Isn't there some way of making them stick to their word?" asked Helen. "Surely, a contract must mean something."

"Oh, of course, there are the law courts," said Ruth as they reached the hotel. "But it is an expensive and tiresome business and a star forced to work against her will can make endless trouble for her concern. It's cheaper to let her go and get some one else."

"But if Viola walks off at the last moment whom will you get?" Helen was persistent and Ruth raised a protesting hand.

"I don't know and I'm not going to think about it, either—not until I've had more proof of Viola's perfidy than we had this morning. I can't afford to borrow trouble."

"If she stops to talk with that fellow much longer she will certainly miss her train," said Helen with a glance at her wrist watch.

CHAPTER 11

TROUBLE IN THE AIR

Ruth was really more worried than she would admit and when Viola appeared at the last minute, looking a bit flurried and out of breath but as cheerful as usual, Ruth drew a long breath of relief. So far, so good, at any rate!

Tom attended to all details in his usual business-like manner and Ruth was grateful to him. The girl could not help wondering at the great change that had come over him since those days when she used to urge him to find a useful occupation and stick to it.

For some reason she was feeling oppressed by worries today. She had not felt that way when she got up in the morning. On the contrary, she had welcomed the thought of Golden Pass and the immediate prospect of getting to work with all her usual enthusiasm. It must be the problem of Viola that was worrying her. That mysterious encounter with Charlie Reid. What could it mean?

However, she felt that once on location with the filming of her picture started, she would be more contented and lose this disturbing feeling of unease that had taken possession of her.

At last the long and tiresome trip was over and they had landed with their belongings on the dismal, almost deserted station of Golden Pass. She looked to see that all her company were present, from the leading actor to the humble, but very important, cameramen, and then turned to Tom with a gesture of weariness.

"I'm so tired, Tom. I'd like to rest for hours and not do a single thing—not even think!"

Tom smiled at her and promptly gave orders for the removal of themselves and their luggage to Headwaters Ranch where they were to stay during the time necessary for the filming of the picture.

Tom and Ruth had gleaned their information concerning this particular ranch from Mr. Hammond. The latter, it seemed, had put up at this ranch during his former stay at Golden Pass and had heartily recommended it to

Ruth and Tom as ideal headquarters for the company during the taking of the picture.

"The ranch is run by a fine old couple," Mr. Hammond had told Tom. "And when I say run, I mean run. One of the finest ranches in the country. I can't promise you luxuries but I can guarantee that Ma Gowdy will furnish you with all the comforts of home. Try it, my boy. You can't go wrong."

Tom had been only too glad to follow this advice. Writing to Headwaters Ranch, he had received a reply by return mail to the effect that the ranch could easily accommodate the number Tom had mentioned in his letter. Since the rates for rooms and meal quoted by the owner of the ranch were satisfactory, Tom, with Ruth's entire sanction and approval, wrote back at once, clinching the deal.

This done, the young fellow drew a long sigh of relief. One of the most vexing problems of the trip had been easily solved, thanks to Mr. Hammond.

Now Tom made inquiries of the young fellows lounging about the station and found that conveyances of a sort had been sent from the ranch.

A good looking, impudent-eyed, rangy lad, had brought a rather dilapidated Ford which, he explained, was for the use of the ladies.

The luggage was to be conveyed in an open wagon driven by one of the other ranch hands. The men, it seemed, were to ride the nervous, velvet-skinned, half-wild colts, kept in hand by a third picturesquely dressed young man.

The eyes of Layton Boardman gleamed as he approached the spirited group of colts. With a soft word or two he reached out and touched the nearest, a caressing movement of hand on velvet nose. The colt trembled but stood still and in a moment the actor's arm stole round the neck of the little beast. Gently he stroked him with his other hand and talked to him softly. With a sudden capitulating whinny the colt rubbed his head against the man's shoulder. It was colt love talk. The two were friends.

Ruth and Helen, watching the little scene with interest, stepped forward eagerly. Even the blasé Viola had stopped talking with the nearest cowboy to watch.

Layton Boardman looked up at the young fellow in charge of the horses.

"Seems like he's mine," he drawled, instinctively dropping back into cowboy dialect. "Just naturally belong together. A beauty, too," rubbing his hand over the sleek coat, "if I know hosses."

"He's full o' ginger, mister," said the youngster, his eyes admiringly on Boardman's breadth of shoulder. One could guess at the man's splendid muscular development, even beneath the conventional, loose-hung suit he wore. "But I guess you can manage him, all right."

"Reckon so," drawled Boardman, and with a lithe movement swung himself into the saddle before even the little colt knew what he was about.

The latter, surprised, reared instinctively in protest, a swift action of rippling muscles and tossing mane that would have given even an experienced rider a moment of tension.

But Boardman clung to the colt's back as easily and with as much nonchalance as though he were reclining in an easy chair at home.

"Now, don't go gettin' all het up," he told the pony in a gentle drawl of reproof. "Ain't a bit of use, little feller. Better sit quiet and save yo' strength," he went on, in true cowboy style.

As though recognizing the wisdom of this advice, the colt set its feet daintily to earth and stood there, pawing the ground.

In the eyes of the cowboys who had gathered around was admiration and, better still, recognition. Layton Boardman was one of them, despite his "swell" clothes and citified air.

"You sho can handle thet colt, mister," one of them said.

"We'll set you to some 'bronco bustin' in a day or two," another shouted.

"Fine," Boardman's eyes gleamed with anticipation. "I'll be there, boys. Just watch me!"

Tom looked at Ruth. She, in turn, was gazing at Layton Boardman, her lips slightly parted with pleasure, eyes bright.

Tom turned away quickly and hurried to oversee the piling of trunks on the wagon. He despised himself for feeling jealous. But this fellow, Boardman, was out of the ordinary. He had magnetism of the sort that draws both men and women to him. Also, Boardman had on his side the glamour that always surrounds an actor. By the time they were ready to start Tom was in a pretty savage mood.

However, the ride to Headwaters Ranch was not one to cultivate moods, except it be one of appreciation of grandeur and beauty in its finest form.

Montana is a land of glorious mountains and fertile valleys, of sunshine and, in the heart of its woodlands, deepest shadow. During that ride along rock mountain roads in the shaky flivver Ruth and Helen saw views unfolding before them that took their breath away, left them in a maze of beauty, groping for adjectives that could describe the things they saw.

How tell others of those lofty mountain peaks, remote and still, towering sentinel-like above the sunlit, pleasant valleys lying fertile and warm at their feet? How describe the picturesque grandeur of the canyons that dropped dizzily away from one's very feet to a dazzling silver ribbon of stream below?

"Ruth, I'm simply steeped in beauty," said Helen after an awed half hour of this. "It was worth coming all the way from Cheslow, if only for a glimpse of this glorious scenery."

"I can see that I'm going to have an embarrassment of riches," said Ruth contentedly. "I'll have to draw lots to decide on locations for my picture."

They came suddenly upon Headwaters Ranch, hiding away between two towering mountains. A stream wound its way through the center of the ranch, making it one of the most fertile in the country.

Ruth gave one glance at the rambling buildings, of the old ranch house itself, and of the sunlit plains back of the house dotted with herds of grazing cattle and immediately forgot all about being tired and her need of rest.

"I've simply got to take a look around before dark!" she told Helen and Tom, as the latter swung from his horse and opened the car door. "I shouldn't wonder if I'd find plenty of material right here on the ranch for my picture."

But since Helen protested that she, at least, was going to make up for some of the sleep she had lost on her travels and Tom urgently advised that Ruth wait until morning for her tour of exploration, the girl finally gave in and followed the others into the house.

There were two old people in charge of the ranch—at least, they would have seemed old to Ruth and Helen had the girls met them in the city. But out here where rugged physique and great endurance are the rule, Ma and Pa Gowdy seemed not so old, as well-seasoned and hardy.

Certain it was that they still ran the ranch with all their old efficiency, hard when it came to demanding every bit of effort from those they employed but just and square in all their dealings with "the boys." Every one loved and was loyal to Pa and Ma Gowdy. The young folks had not been long on the ranch before they realized that Ma, good old sport that she was, had equal say in the management of the ranch with Pa—and desertions and insurrection were practically unheard of on Headwaters Ranch.

Pa, they learned upon entering the house, was out on the ranch somewhere, but Ma had waited to greet her guests.

She was a tall, powerfully built woman, dressed in uncompromising calico that failed to detract from her air of quiet forcefulness.

She looked at the company, seeming in one, quick canny glance to take in every detail of it, then led the way quietly into the big front room. Somehow Ruth gathered that Ma Gowdy was almost always silent.

"I'm Ruth Fielding," said Ruth as the old lady turned to face them. She introduced the others and to each introduction Ma Gowdy nodded gravely, neither speaking nor smiling.

"I suppose what you all want, really, is to get to your rooms and clean up some," she said when the introductions were over. "Andy here," motioning to an embarrassed youth in the doorway, "will show you where you're to stay. I reckon you'll find everything ready for you. If you want anything, all

51

you have to do is stick your head out the door and call out. We're plain folks, but I hope you'll be comfortable while you stay. Supper'll be ready in 'bout an hour."

She turned and left them then to the care of Andy, who seemed not at all certain what to do with his arms and legs. He used the latter finally as a means of locomotion, and succeeded in assigning the leading members of the company to large, rather scantily furnished rooms on the second floor.

Viola was heard to comment audibly on the bareness of her quarters and to yearn in homesick tones for the comfort of her "bung-ul-ow."

Ruth was about to shut the door to her own particular apartment when Helen pushed her way in.

"Ruth, I've got one room too many," she complained. "The place that ridiculous Andy gave me is big enough for sixteen people. Do have a heart —though I have reason to believe you haven't—and let me come in with you."

Ruth chuckled and glanced at the enormous bedstead in one corner of the room.

"There certainly is room enough for two," she admitted. "Did you ever see such a big barn of a place?"

But, though the room was big and bare enough, the view from the windows of it was more than enough to compensate. Arms about each other, the two girls stood at the largest of the three windows, drinking in the beauty of the sun-flecked range, dotted by innumerable grazing cattle, with, beyond and above it, the towering, misty peaks of the mountains.

"That's the Rocky Mountain range, isn't it?" said Helen dreamily. "There ought to be good hunting up in those woods, Ruthie."

"Plenty of deer, I suppose," agreed Ruth. "But I hate to think of any one's hunting them for sport—beautiful, soft-eyed things."

"Well, I don't suppose you can keep Tom away from it. I know he packed his rifle along and he'll probably spend every spare minute he can get using it."

"I wish he'd left his old rifle at home," said Ruth crossly. "We didn't come up here to hunt."

Helen's prophecy proved correct. The next morning Tom put on outing clothes and took his rifle, declaring his intention of browsing about a bit.

"I may bring back only a rabbit," he told them. "Deer is out of season. But they say rabbit is very good to eat, cooked the way these westerners know how to cook them."

"Don't stay too long, will you, Tom?" asked Ruth, with just a touch of coldness in her voice. "I want to look for locations before long, you know."

"You won't need me until noon, will you?" he asked.

"No—and probably not then," said Ruth, turning away with a little shrug of her shoulder.

"If Tom would rather go hunting than stay around and do his part in the preliminary work of the picture, he can go hunting and stay as long as he wants to!" Ruth told herself defiantly. "I don't care what he does!"

And Tom, not knowing that she was piqued and hurt, gave her a curious look, hesitated, then turned and swung off in the direction of the woods, his rifle slung over his shoulder.

He had gone only a few feet when it occurred to him that he had better enter those unfamiliar woods on horseback.

"The ponies know these mountain trails better than I—at least, they're more sure-footed," he told himself, and turned toward the corrals.

Ruth saw to it that the members of her company were well employed. Some of them had not finished reading the script. Others set out afoot or on horseback to explore the country. Viola and Layton Boardman had already gone for a morning canter.

All her small duties attended to, Ruth felt free at last to go about her own business. And that business was, first of all, to explore Headwaters Ranch thoroughly.

She and Helen selected ponies from the corrals and set forth on a brisk canter. The ranch lands were even more picturesque close to than they had been when seen in perspective from the window.

Ma and Pa Gowdy did no farming—at least, not more than enough to supply their own needs. The fertile lands were given over almost completely to stock raising.

"I never saw so many animals in my life," said Helen. The herds of cattle fascinated her and frightened her at the same time. "I think I'll go back, if you don't mind, Ruthie dear. Yonder big steer has a mean and hungry eye."

Ruth laughed absently.

"All right. I'll be coming along in a little while. I want to go as far as the stream and see what it looks like—if I can make it before noon."

Ruth scarcely knew when Helen left her. Her mind was glowing with the realization that many of her scenes in her scenario could be shot right here on the ranch. She dismounted from her horse and led it lightly by the bridle. Such local color, such background!

She was roused from her dreaming by a strange sound as of the distant pounding of surf upon the shore. Even as she lifted her head with a swift, startled motion the sound became louder and swelled to a roar of pounding hoofs.

Ruth looked and her heart leaped wildly. Down upon her, started probably by some imaginary thing, swept a solid sea of steers, heads tossing,

53

hoofs tearing at the turf. And in the path of this dreadful wave Ruth stood, unable to move, unable even to cry aloud.

CHAPTER 12

IN PERIL

Ruth's pony snorted in terror. With a toss of its head, the animal reared backward, almost losing its balance, then galloped wildly back toward the corrals.

Ruth was living through a nightmare. She tried to move, but found that her legs would not respond to her command. What use to run, anyway, when there was no possible hope of escape? She felt numb, frozen with terror.

Muffled by the thunder of pounding hoofs she did not hear the rider approaching from behind, was not aware of him until a horse swung up beside her, all plunging hoofs and waving mane.

Layton Boardman leaned wide of his horse, swept an arm toward Ruth.

"Into the saddle—quick!" he shouted. "One chance left!"

It was a magnificent gesture and would have been successful had not the pony, maddened by terror, reared on its hind feet, flinging over backward.

Boardman was not prepared for the sudden motion, was flung from his saddle and sprawled motionless on the ground. Ruth moaned.

That horrible sea of steers was almost upon them. In a moment she would be lying there, too!

Came the noise of shouting behind her. A shot cracked out and the nearest steer fell, kicking and plowing up the turf.

Another report and another. Other steers fell, and those rushing up behind stumbled over them and fell, a kicking, snorting mass. Something was wrong. The packed mass of steers wavered, hesitated, then divided and swept on in two great trampling streams.

Ruth watched them in a daze, so numbed with fear that for a moment she scarcely realized she was safe.

Then Tom was beside her, Tom's arms about her, steadying her, Tom's voice, gruff and anxious:

"You aren't hurt, Ruth? You're all right?"

She nodded. Then lifted her white face to him.

"Did you—were you the one who fired the shots?"

"One of the ones," he replied, modest as always. "For the rest you'll have to thank these boys. They sure are classy marksmen."

Then, for the first time, Ruth saw the group of cowboys that had surrounded them in sympathetic interest. She drew away from Tom selfconsciously and looked toward Layton Boardman.

The latter had got to his feet. Blood flowed from a wound on his forehead where he had struck a stone in falling and he swayed so dizzily that one of the cowboys put an arm about his shoulders to support him.

"I'm all right," said the actor, evidently impatient with himself for allowing the horse to throw him. "Never mind about me, lad."

He tried to take a step forward, brought up, amazed, while his face went white with pain.

Ruth stepped forward involuntarily.

"What is it? Are you hurt?" she cried.

Boardman shook his head and tried to smile, but the corners of his mouth twitched painfully.

"Not much, I guess. Just some trouble with my ankle. All right—in a minute—" He tried to step again, but once more drew up and dubiously shook his head.

"Can't do it, boys. Any one got a hoss that ain't working?"

There were a dozen offers, for the cowboys were thoroughly beneath the spell of Layton Boardman. The latter was able with only slight aid to swing himself to the back of one of the ponies. He sat there, one foot in the stirrup, the other dangling, as fine a picture of wounded hero as one would wish to see.

Ruth walked over to his pony's side and put her hand up frankly.

"I want to thank you for what you tried to do for me," she said softly. "I want you to know that I fully appreciate it."

Boardman grasped the proffered hand and met Ruth's friendly glance with a direct one of his own.

"To see you safe," he said simply, "is all the thanks I need."

Then he was gone, surrounded by a group of cowboys.

Ruth's horse had been rounded up and brought back to her. She mounted silently, feeling weak and exhausted after her terrifying experience.

Tom mounted also and they started back toward the ranch.

Suppose Layton Boardman, their leading man, were badly hurt? Men had been permanently lamed by no worse an accident than he had had, and it would be impossible to get another in his place this late—not for a considerable time, at any rate.

And, in the meantime, even delay might be serious, with Viola drawing her salary whether she worked or not, as did, for that matter, all the rest of them.

Oh, well, Ruth shrugged off the weight of anxiety. Boardman would probably be all right in a day or two. Only a slight sprain probably.

She looked at Tom, jogging along silently beside her. He looked tired and very grave and suddenly her heart smote her. Why, she had never even thanked him for his very important part in her rescue!

"Tom," she said, "it was magnificent of you to do what you did!"

He looked up, surprised.

"I couldn't have done anything else," he said quietly.

CHAPTER 13

NEW WORRIES

It was the day after her adventure with the stampeding cattle and Ruth was taking a morning of rest before starting once more on a hunt for suitable locations.

The two girls, Helen and Ruth, were up in Ruth's room which various soft and colorful articles from their trunks had made livable, talking over plans for the picture and Ruth's almost miraculous escape the day before. At least, Ruth was trying to talk of her picture and Helen could not be deflected from the theme of Ruth's adventure, which interested her vividly.

"Just think, only a little thing like chance or fate or whatever you call it kept me from being there myself," Helen observed. "I had a horror of those savage looking steers."

"It's nothing to what I have now," said Ruth, with a reminiscent shudder.

"But think of the romance!" Helen was not to be stopped. "Think of having Layton Boardman save you!"

"He didn't," said Ruth dryly.

"Well, he tried to, which is the same thing," Helen said in a tone of reproach. Ruth chuckled.

"It isn't at all the same kind of thing, I assure you," she retorted, "as you would very well realize if you had been in my shoes."

"Well, you had Tom, anyway, and a whole raft of cowboys, when Boardman got kicked by his horse."

"He didn't get kicked by a horse! How many times do I have to tell you?" Ruth laid down her papers in despair and Helen smiled mischievously at her.

"I knew I'd make you stop working by fair means or foul," she said shamelessly.

"And I don't feel like working—not a little bit," Ruth confessed. "I'd just like to let go—for a little while, anyway."

"Well, why don't you? Every one has to rest sometimes, you know, even Ruth Fielding, whether she knows it or not. Here, take a chocolate and give me a full and complete account of yesterday."

"But I don't want to talk about yesterday," Ruth objected, accepting the candy. "I tell you, if you had been there you wouldn't be so keen on the subject."

"Poor Ruthie!" Helen reached over and patted her chum's hand. "You did have a dreadful shaking up. Wasn't it lucky that Tom happened to be coming home just then?"

"It was very lucky," sighed Ruth, resigning herself to a discussion of the subject since Helen, quite evidently, could be induced to talk of nothing else. "I certainly wasn't much use myself. I couldn't move a finger."

There was a short silence while Ruth dreamed over plans for her picture and Helen reviewed mentally the events of the day before.

"I suppose Tom was put out to find handsome Layton on the ground before him," said Helen, and Ruth shook herself impatiently.

"Layton, as you call him, was certainly on the ground most literally," she said, with a frown. "And I don't know whether you know that my interest in his injury is far more professional than personal."

Helen nodded.

"I suppose you mean that having him laid up may delay your picture."

"That's certainly what I do mean!" Ruth sat up energetically and began to look more like her old fighting self. "It seems to me that there's an evil sprite following me this trip—"

"Have you been to see him yet?"

Ruth shook her head.

"I was going to pretty soon. Tell you the truth," she looked at Helen seriously, "I'm almost afraid to. I'm so afraid that he may have something more than a sprained ankle, and then—" She shrugged her shoulders eloquently.

"A good many of the pictures can be taken without him, can't they?" asked Helen sympathetically. "Pictures where he doesn't appear?"

"A few. But he appears in most of them. He plays a very strong lead all through. Of course," she stopped to consider, "we could take pictures of the rodeo and the avalanche—"

"Oh, are we really going to have an avalanche?" Helen's eyes sparkled. "What fun!"

"An avalanche!" repeated Ruth. "Why, of course. That's the main part of the picture."

Helen was leaning forward now, alert and eager.

"It will be artificial, of course?"

Ruth smiled.

"We could hardly ask Mother Nature to give us a special demonstration as a favor," she said. "Of course the avalanche will be the result of carefully planted dynamite. But it will be as real looking as ingenuity can make it."

"I'll count on you for that," said Helen, regarding her chum admiringly. "But I really didn't know we were going to have anything so exciting. Isn't it—" she paused and regarded her friend uncertainly, "isn't it a bit dangerous?"

"A certain amount of danger always attaches to anything like that," said Ruth carelessly. "There are always a lot of unforeseen things that may happen. Still, we've taken every possible precaution, and that's the best we can do."

"Cost a heap of money I suppose?" said Helen, after another short pause. Ruth nodded.

"More than I care to think about. Which reminds me that I must have a business talk with Tom tonight and find out just how we stand. I, personally, have some dead steers to pay for, too, I suppose," and the girl sighed.

"I don't see why 'personally.' You didn't kill the steers."

"No; but they were killed in my cause."

"I think Tom will look after that in spite of your hands-off independence. You don't treat Tommy-boy right, Ruthie."

Ruth made no response to this observation, and the girls were silent for a while.

"Seen anything suspicious about Viola lately?" asked Helen as Ruth sorted out her papers and put them away.

"No, and I'm letting a sleeping dog lie," replied Ruth emphatically.

"With all apologies to Viola," chuckled Helen.

"I've about come to the conclusion," Ruth added as she got up and began to straighten her hair before the mirror over the washstand, "that her conference with Bloomberg's agent didn't mean anything. I have enough trouble without worrying about that."

"It isn't your worrying that matters," observed Helen. "It's what Viola does."

"Oh, well, we'll let the matter rest. As a matter of fact, so far, Viola has done nothing wrong. I suppose I'm too suspicious."

"Where are you going?" asked Helen as Ruth turned toward the door.

"Over to see Layton Boardman," said Ruth, with a faint smile. "I've got to know the worst."

"I'd offer to come, too," Helen's lazy teasing voice floated out after her, "if I were not perfectly well aware that three's a crowd."

Ruth shrugged impatiently. She wished others would stop being so foolish about her and Layton Boardman. The whole thing was ridiculous.

She went to Boardman's door and knocked. He called to her to come in. She opened the door and entered the room, leaving the door open behind her.

The actor was in bed, but as Ruth entered a quick smile played over his white face. Ruth went to him quickly and took the hand he had stretched impulsively toward her.

"I'm sorry you were hurt," she said, bending over him solicitously. "Is there anything that I can do?"

It chanced that at that moment Tom was passing through the hall in search of Ruth. He saw her hand in Layton Boardman's, saw the girl bending over him.

With a grim tightening of his lips Tom went on past the door and down the hall.

CHAPTER 14

HELEN IS HURT

Besides the injury to his ankle, which was comparatively light, being only a painful sprain, Layton Boardman had hurt his back in his fall. This, together with painful bruises about the head and body, had prompted the ranch doctor to order him to stay in bed for a few days.

"After that I'll be fit as a fiddle again," Boardman told Ruth, trying to reassure her. "If you can shoot some of the pictures that don't show me, Miss Fielding—"

"Don't worry, Mr. Boardman," Ruth cut in to his anxious sentence. "We'll go right ahead. There will be several days of hard work anyway before we'll need you. And whatever happens, I want you to take plenty of time and get perfectly well. The scenes where you do come in," she added with a smile, "are pretty strenuous, you know, and you'll need all your strength."

Boardman groaned and moved his aching body impatiently.

"I wanted to take part in the rodeo. I wanted it more than I've wanted anything in years. And now—look at me!"

"I'm sorry," said Ruth reluctantly, "but I'm afraid we will have to shoot that without you."

Boardman turned suddenly and caught Ruth's hand in his hard, sinewy one.

"Promise me one thing," he begged. "Promise me you'll put off the rodeo as long as you can. I may possibly be in shape!"

Ruth promised and withdrew her hand gently.

"Now rest a little while and I'll go down and see if Ma Gowdy will let me make you a little chicken broth for your dinner. That ought to help put you in shape for the rodeo."

"You're very good to me," Boardman muttered and closed his eyes.

Ma Gowdy was in the kitchen and readily responded to Ruth's request for chicken broth for the invalid.

"There's one fresh-killed," she told Ruth. "A fat, tough old fowl that will make fine soup. You leave it to me. I can see you have plenty on your mind."

Ruth thanked her gratefully and went on out.

She had already consulted with Pa Gowdy and found him perfectly will-ing that she use his ranch and as many of his ranch hands as she could muster in her great scene of the rodeo. She wanted now to find out just how many of these boys she could depend upon.

She found Andy, the gangling lad who helped in the small truck garden at the rear of the house and who also did chores for Ma Gowdy in the house. There were two regular cooks in Ma's kitchen, swarthy Mexicans, both of them, but Andy was general utility man.

This handy youth took her to the foreman of the ranch who was at that moment watching a spirited exhibition of bronco busting in the corral.

This fellow, a long, lean, blue-eyed man whose face seemed to break up into a million tiny wrinkles when he smiled, received Ruth cordially.

"I think you'll find, Miss, that the only trouble you'll have will be in get-tin' too many volunteers," he assured her when she stated her errand. "The boys is more interested in this here movin' picture outfit of yours these days than in anything else that goes on about the ranch. They think this here rodeo you're stagin' is a regular game. You'll have no trouble gettin' them to take part."

The man proved a true prophet. Ruth's only difficulty was in rejecting in such a way as to spare their feelings the cowboys she could not use.

"But I can't take you all!" she protested. "Pa and Ma Gowdy would run me off the ranch if I took you all from your regular work. I must pick and choose."

It was not long before her list was full. She gave her new extras explicit directions as to where and at what time on the following morning she wanted them, and then she went to find and instruct her cameramen.

Ruth had pretty clearly in mind what she wanted. There had been a rodeo once not far from Cheslow and she had watched the antics of the cowboys with thrilled interest. It was her ambition to have this pictured rodeo as near like the genuine article as she could make it.

There would be bronco busting, of course. This was to be the main event of the affair. Then there would be a race, three or four half-broken colts let loose in a restricted area. Into the ring would dash a mounted cowboy in spectacular fashion. It was the business of this particular participant to chase the half wild horses and, coming close to one of them, to leap to its back, landing there, if the Fates were kind, and hold on grimly until such time as the next horse came within leaping distance, when the process was to be repeated.

In the course of this exciting performance falls and accidents, sometimes serious accidents, were to be expected. Perhaps this, thought Ruth, with a wry grimace, was what supplied the thrill. At any rate, there was bound to be plenty of excitement and action, and this was what she must have in her picture.

There would be other events, too, including the roping of steers.

"I wanted," she told Helen, a frown of anxiety furrowing her brow, "to have Layton Boardman himself take the lead in the events requiring skill in the use of the lariat. That is one of his strong points."

Both girls knew how nonchalantly and well Boardman could manage the snakelike, almost magic rope, twisting, turning, etching strange, serpentine figures on the air and always in the end finding the mark it was meant for.

Ruth had pictured Boardman in these scenes of her scenario, knew how his fine personality would dominate them. There were other cowboys no doubt who had his skill with the lariat, but none that could borrow that intangible thing—his personality.

"Well, the best you can do is to shoot most of the scenes tomorrow—those in which Boardman's not absolutely necessary—and take the others when your leading man is on his feet again," said Helen, then went to her room to write to Chess.

Ruth had an interview with her cameramen in which location and light effects were discussed at length, then went to consult her scenario as to the exact sequence of scenes.

In the hall she met Viola Callahan and the latter stared at Ruth, a queer expression in her bold black eyes.

"Seems like your hero's kind of laid down on his job," she remarked flippantly to Ruth. "I can't imagine myself in love with a wild-west chap who gets his back wrenched and an ankle hurt right at the beginning of things. Right poor judgment, I call it."

"You may remember that Mr. Boardman injured himself trying to save my life," Ruth answered coldly, and went on up to her room wondering why she disliked this girl so much. Disliked her—and distrusted her, too.

Viola had given Ruth no cause for distrust other than that meeting in Chicago with Sol Bloomberg's agent. Ruth had to admit that. Since her arrival at the ranch Viola's actions had been normal enough. Yet Ruth still distrusted her with a suspicion that was as inevitable as the drawing of her breath.

Again she thrust uneasy thoughts from her. She would not borrow trouble.

The different events of the rodeo had been practiced for days—bronco busting, racing, bull-throwing. The cowboys had entered into the acting with spirit, even though most of it was not acting to them at all, but merely a part of their everyday experience.

The time had now come when Ruth felt that she could safely set up her cameras and shoot the scenes.

The day of the rodeo dawned gloriously clear and one fear of Ruth's was dissipated. At least they would not be forced to postpone the rodeo pictures because of bad weather.

"Oh, Ruth!" exclaimed Helen, standing at the open window. "It's a perfectly grand day. I'm so glad it isn't raining, or even cloudy."

Dressed and ready for the exciting events of the day, Ruth stopped for a moment at Boardman's door. The latter was better. He had insisted on getting out of bed and was now sitting comfortably enough propped up in a big chair by the window. He looked up as Ruth entered and smiled.

She outlined to him her general plans concerning the rodeo, explaining that she had saved several of the most important and daring scenes for him.

"That was mighty good of you!" There was no doubting his gratitude. "I'll be up and around as good as new in a day or two. Just watch me!"

Ruth said she certainly hoped he would and left him and ran buoyantly down the steps and into the vigorous, sun-dazzled out-of-doors.

She found Tom and Helen waiting for her.

"Oh, here you are!" cried Helen. "Tom and I have been waiting hours!"

"Nothing of the kind," laughed Ruth happily. "I left you not more than five minutes ago."

The cameramen and a group of eager extras stood near by.

The cowboys regarded Ruth with dancing eyes and demanded to know when the show was to begin.

"Right away," said Ruth. "The sooner the better. Is everybody ready?"

It seemed that everybody was, and they repaired straightway to location.

From then on events moved so swiftly that Ruth lost all account of time. Close to the cameramen, ordering, criticizing, directing and sometimes giving voice to spontaneous expressions of approval, Ruth seemed to dominate the whole exciting scene with her own vivid personality.

The cowboys afterward declared that they worked their best because of the director's enthusiasm and intense vitality.

"With her dancin' away there on her little toes and shoutin' herself hoarse when we done somethin' she liked, we just couldn't help playin' up good," said one of these, thereby expressing the general opinion, for there was a murmured chorus of:

"Now you've said something, buddy."

At any rate, up to the final "shot" Ruth was confident that she had a smashing good picture, the real thing in a real setting, a far more realistic rodeo than even she had ever dreamed of filming.

There was one event left—the steer roping. Since this was to be the climactic event of the rodeo it was to start with a roar and a bang, the boys shooting revolvers into the air not only for the purpose of exciting their already over-nervous mounts but to provoke the steers to a fighting mood which would make even the most skillful lariat throwing and roping a difficult undertaking.

Helen stood a little way from Tom and Ruth, tense with excitement and interest. This was the sort of thing that thrilled Helen to her toes, as she expressed it, and she was eager to miss no slightest detail of the event.

Tom, too, was full of enthusiasm and also of his old wondering admiration of Ruth. He was more like the old Tom than he had been for many a day. Even through the general excitement Ruth was aware of this change in his attitude and was happy because of it.

Then the scene was set, the outdoor stage was ready for its actors. A steer, a great, angry-looking old fellow, was let loose.

With wild whoops and shouts the boys dashed forward, firing their revolvers into the air as they went. The noise was terrific, the excitement tense.

Ruth, exhilarated and excited, turned to look at Helen, saw the girl throw up her hands in a startled gesture, saw her reel and fall limp to the ground!

"Helen! Oh, Helen!" moaned Ruth.

CHAPTER 15

STARTLING NEWS

Together, Ruth and Tom rushed over to the prone figure on the ground. They seemed to be the only ones of all that company to see the accident to Helen.

The cowboys, engrossed in the swift action and the excitement of the scene, all lesser sounds drowned by their wild cries and shouts, saw nothing. The cameramen continued to grind out length after length of film, oblivious to everything save the drama of the scene before them.

"Is she dead?" gasped Ruth to Tom, as they bent over the girl.

It was here that Ruth's training in the Red Cross stood her in good stead. She knelt beside Helen, took her wrist in expert fingers. Though her face was white and drawn, her voice was calm and controlled as she spoke to Tom.

"She's breathing, but her pulse is weak. We must get her into the house at once, Tom!"

"Some fool forgot to put blank cartridges in his gun," muttered Tom, hands clenched.

Together they got the unconscious girl to the house. Ma Gowdy met them at the door and led them, with no waste of words, into the living room where they laid Helen on the couch.

Blood was flowing from a wound on her forehead. Ruth spoke to the capable old woman and Ma Gowdy disappeared kitchenward.

Meanwhile Ruth had been loosening Helen's clothes, tearing the tie and collar of her blouse away from her throat, chafing her hands. Ruth's face was almost as white as that of her chum.

"Tom, if anything has happened to her—through me—"

Just then Ma Gowdy came back with clean strips of linen and a basin of water.

With a brief word of thanks, Ruth seized the basin of water and the strips of linen. Ma Gowdy watched with approval while Ruth set to work carefully bathing and cleansing the wound on Helen's forehead.

"Only a scalp wound," she murmured, after a moment. "Oh, I feared it might be much, much worse!"

"How'd it happen?" asked Ma Gowdy.

"Spent bullet," Tom responded briefly. He had taken one of his sister's hands in his and was rubbing it gently. "Some fool had real bullets instead of the blank cartridges I ordered. I intend," he added grimly, "to find out who that fool was, and without delay."

The scalp wound thoroughly cleansed, Ruth took one of the clean strips of linen, dipped it in the icy cold water, and bathed Helen's face with it. The girl opened her eyes, looked up languidly.

Then she shivered and put a hand to her bandaged forehead.

"I feel like a wreck," she said with a faint smile, and closed her eyes again.

Suddenly and for no apparent reason, Ruth burst into tears. She turned away, fumbled for a handkerchief, and the next moment felt Tom's big one thrust into her hand. She accepted it gratefully, wiped her eyes, and smiled at him.

"I'm such an awful goose!" she said. "But I thought she was going to die!"

The next moment she was beside Helen again, stroking her hair back from her poor throbbing forehead and telling her not to talk but just to rest until she felt stronger.

For a few moments the new patient lay quiet, seemingly content beneath Ruth's gentle ministrations. But suddenly she stirred restlessly and half sat up.

Ruth pushed her back gently and Helen's eyes flew open. She regarded her chum resentfully.

"If you think I'm going to lie here, Ruth Fielding," she announced with something of her old vigor, "you are very much mistaken!"

"Behave yourself, sis." Tom's voice was gentle, but there was an underlying firmness that Helen generally obeyed. "Right where you are is where you're going to stay—for the rest of this day, at least."

Helen stared at them both for a moment, looked at Ma Gowdy hovering in the background, hesitated as though contemplating rebellion, then, with a sigh, gave in.

"What hit me?" she asked, moving her aching head restlessly. "I felt as though somebody had touched me with a red hot poker. Then I didn't feel anything."

Ruth explained and Tom declared his intention of sallying forth immediately for the purpose of finding out what idiot carried real cartridges in his revolver.

"You take charge of everything, Tom," Ruth called after him. "Tell the boys we won't want them any more today. We were nearly through anyway, and if we have to retake the last event tomorrow it won't matter, although I don't think it will be necessary. I'll stay here with Helen."

"I don't see why you have to stop everything on my account," said Helen. "You make me feel guilty, Ruthie."

"Of course you were responsible for getting hit," Ruth gibed. "If you only knew," she knelt down beside Helen and took her hand gently, "what a relief it was to find you were not seriously hurt! For a minute I thought— But there, we're not going to talk about it—either of us. You just turn over like a good girl, with your face to the wall, and get some sleep."

"Suppose I can't sleep?"

"Then I'll read to you till you do."

Although nothing very serious came of Helen's accident, Ruth was careful to keep her chum in the background after that whenever there was a shooting scene to be taken. Luckily, the cameramen, having been too engrossed in their work to notice the accident to Helen, had kept on grinding and the great final scene of the rodeo had not been lost.

Tom made careful inquiries and found that, as he expected, one of the boys had forgotten to exchange real cartridges for blank ones in his weapon. When told what his carelessness had done the young fellow was so overwhelmed with genuine remorse that Tom considered he had received punishment enough. That one cowboy, at least, would be very careful in the future!

Ruth received a letter from Mr. Hammond a day or two after the accident, announcing his intention of stopping at Golden Pass for a brief visit on his way farther west.

Ruth was delighted at the prospect, for aside from the fact that she was always glad to see her old friend and business associate she set a high value on his criticism. It always gave her a feeling of content and certainty when Mr. Hammond's judgment backed up hers.

In the meantime, Layton Boardman had made good his promise of rapid convalescence. He was up and around the day after the pictures of the rodeo, hobbling a bit painfully, but otherwise appearing up to his usual form. He had recovered, at any rate, to such an extent that he was able to "fake" some close-up scenes before the camera. Ruth had hopes that before long her leading man would be able to take part in two of the important events of the rodeo that had been delayed for his benefit.

Meanwhile Ruth kept her company busy rehearsing for the small scenes. She was anxious to finish the filming of her picture, for expenses were mounting and salaries ate into the business bank roll alarmingly.

Came the time when everything was in readiness for the taking of the first small scene. Ruth, flushed and weary, had rehearsed, directed, cajoled and bullied until she felt that at last she had pulled the company into perfect shape.

"I haven't a bit of pep left in me," she confessed to Tom and Helen that night after dinner. "I feel like a wet dishrag. All I want is to get to bed and sleep forever."

"You'll feel differently in the morning," Helen assured her, while she studied her friend with laughing, quizzical eyes. "I never saw any one like you, Ruth Fielding. No matter how exhausted you may seem at night, morning finds you as fresh and as hungry for new worlds to conquer as ever. I don't see how you manage it."

"It's fun—all of it," Ruth responded, her eyes sparkling in spite of fatigue. "Those scenes ought to go splendidly. If only," a shadow crossed her face, "Viola will behave herself and not try to hog all the scenes."

Tom, who had been lounging at the open window, turned and faced the two girls.

"How about Boardman?" he asked. "Do you think he will be able to disguise his limp well enough to fool the camera?"

Ruth nodded confidently.

"I'm not worrying a bit about Layton."

"I wish," said Tom, grim and enigmatic but sufficiently clear to both Helen and Ruth, "I could say the same!"

Morning came, and with it, as Helen had prophesied, a return of Ruth's enthusiasm and vitality. She went about the preparations for the day's work eagerly, gathering her company about her, reminding, instructing, abjuring.

When everything was in readiness Ruth looked about her, searching for a familiar black-eyed face that certainly should be there.

"Where's Viola?" she asked impatiently. "She must know we are ready to start!"

"I'll go and hunt her up," Tom volunteered, but Ruth shook her head.

"I'll go," she said and there was a glint of something more than determination in her eyes. "If she thinks," she added to herself as she went hurriedly toward the house, "that she can keep every one waiting like this she'll soon find her mistake. If only," she mused half humorously, "we directors were spared the problem of dealing with the whims and fancies of our temperamental stars, how simple everything would be. Anyway," she smiled whimsically, "I'll show this one that if I haven't much temperament I've plenty of temper!"

She reached Viola's door, knocked on it gently. When there was no response she knocked again. After the third attempt she tried the knob of the door and, finding that it turned easily, opened the door and entered the room.

What she saw there made her gasp with a swift premonition of disaster.

Dresser drawers stood open as though the result of a hasty packing. Viola's trunk that had stood in one corner of the room had been dragged to the center. On the top of the trunk was a sheet of paper, scrawled across with Viola's windy writing.

Ruth picked up the paper and as through a blur read the words:

"Sorry, but Tony and I are going over to Bloomberg. Bloomberg's making it worth my while and I'd be a fool if I didn't take my chance while it's offered. You will have to get some one in my place."

CHAPTER 16

AN INCREDIBLE SUGGESTION

That was all. Ruth stood staring at the words dumbly while the true meaning of them filtered into her numbed brain.

Viola had gone, jumped her contract, left at a time when she knew her leaving would be utterly disastrous to the picture.

The thought roused the girl to a sort of wild disbelief. It wasn't so. It couldn't be so! Why, it would mean the ruin not only of this picture, but perhaps of The Fielding Film Company as well.

It was a new company, ambitious and, up to this time, almost incredibly successful. But to make the kind of pictures Ruth wanted to make took money—big lumps of it—and until profits began to be felt from the last big picture, "Snowblind," it was necessary for Ruth to trim her sails very neatly and sail close to the wind if she hoped to avoid shipwreck.

All these thoughts and more, many more, whirled through her brain in that brief moment of realization. She felt faint and sick with the shock.

Viola's note still clasped in her fingers, she went to her own room and sat down in a chair by the window to think things out. She hoped no one would follow just then—not even Tom. To be alone was what she needed—to think things out!

Poor Ruth! The more she tried to think things out the more she came to the realization that there was no way out save a disastrous one.

Even if she and Tom succeeded in getting an actress to take Viola's place, the undertaking would entail ruinous delay. And at this late moment it would be hard to find any one capable of taking the lead in Ruth's picture who was not already bound by contract.

"Oh, it's hopeless—utterly hopeless!" she said, at last, aloud. "I guess fate is against you this time, Ruth Fielding. You might as well acknowledge the defeat as gracefully as you can. Oh, I feel so tired!" She got up and went wearily over to the window. "And how my head does ache!"

From the window she could see a considerable distance down the road. She noticed, in a detached and impersonal way that a conveyance of some kind was jouncing along the dusty trail coming toward the ranch.

She watched it disinterestedly, her mind busy with its own disquieting thoughts. Then as an automobile turned into the road that led to the house her interest quickened.

Who could be riding to the ranch in all the dignity of a car? Almost certainly a stranger, for the natives used horseflesh almost exclusively as a mode of travel.

The figure in gray descending from the car was familiar. Ruth leaned forward, the stranger turned his face toward her, and the next moment she recognized Mr. Hammond.

Why, of course! How could she have forgotten? She had known his arrival to be imminent, had even considered the probability that he would reach the ranch today.

A wry little smile touched the corners of Ruth's mouth. What a different greeting she could have given him had he come an hour, yes, even half an hour before!

She was happy then, exhilarated, excited, could have shown him about with pride. Now!

Still watching him, she saw Mr. Hammond turn in greeting and saw that Tom was coming toward the house on a run. They clasped hands eagerly, for the two were friends. Ruth turned from the window, a lump in her throat. It was dreadful to have to shatter their pleasure and happiness with her bad news.

However, it was Ruth's rule that if anything unpleasant was to be done, the only sensible procedure was to do it at once and get the agony over with.

She straightened her shoulders, instinctively bracing herself, and went on downstairs to greet the new arrival.

They were on the porch and Mr. Hammond turned to her with genuine eagerness.

"My dear Miss Ruth, what a pleasure to see you again. And how splendid you look! Doesn't she?" turning with a smile to Tom.

But Tom had been watching Ruth's face and, sensitive as he was to all her moods, saw instantly that something was wrong.

"What happened?" he asked quietly.

Ruth gave a queer little laugh and dropped into one of the chairs on the porch, motioning them to do likewise.

"I hate to spoil your first minute with us, Mr. Hammond, but this is so dreadful—" She broke off and then fairly flung her next words at Tom. "Viola is gone. All she left is—this!" And with a little despairing gesture she handed the note to Tom.

The latter read it and, still without speaking, passed it to Mr. Hammond.

The latter looked concerned, took a long breath, and cleared his throat.

"Pretty bad, pretty bad," he murmured. "Hadn't you a contract?" he asked of Ruth.

The girl raised her hands and let them drop again, helplessly.

"Of course. But what good does that do in a case like this? If we did succeed in holding her she would probably repay us by giving the worst acting she has. And the heroine's part is a dramatic one, as you know. Indifferent acting would completely spoil the whole picture."

"And whatever one may think of Viola personally, one has to admit she can act," muttered Tom. His gaze roamed out past the ranch lands to Golden Pass. His hands gripped the arm of his chair. "I can't for the life of me see any way out of this!" he added hopelessly.

"There's always a way out of every situation," said Mr. Hammond slowly, a thoughtful look coming into his eyes.

"Always," agreed Ruth. "But sometimes it is anything but a good way."

"Oh, come, Miss Ruth," said the president of the Alectrion Film Corporation, "I've been in this game longer than you have and have weathered many a squall, some as bad as this."

After this speech there was silence on the porch for several minutes.

"Meanwhile," said Ruth, rousing herself to thought of the present, "I suppose the entire company is waiting the coming of its director—and Viola. We'll have to tell them, there's no use waiting, Tom."

"So we shall." Tom rose heavily and, hands thrust deep in pockets, sauntered to the piazza steps. There he turned and with an effort grinned at Mr. Hammond.

"I'd ask you to excuse my absence if I thought you'd miss me," he said.

"Now what did he mean by that?" asked Ruth, looking after him.

"Probably that you and I may have something to say to each other," laughed Mr. Hammond. "And, as far as I'm concerned," he added, with a change of tone that made Ruth look at him swiftly, "he's dead right."

Ruth said nothing, only continued to look at Mr. Hammond, her heart beating faster. She felt that he was leading up to something. What was it?

"You may not like what I have to say, Miss Ruth." The man was looking away from her now, speaking slowly, distinctly. "But I've got to say it for all that." He turned to her with his quick disarming smile. "As a matter of fact, I think that I see a very satisfactory way out of your difficulties."

"You do?" Ruth gasped. She was staring at him incredulously.

"I believe it is only your modesty that keeps you from thinking of it yourself," went on Hammond.

"I don't know what you mean!" Ruth was eager now, expectant. "Please, please don't keep me in suspense!"

"Then I won't."

Mr. Hammond leaned toward her. The easy smile had left his face. He spoke in all seriousness.

"You are a scenario writer of unusual ability, Miss Ruth, and a good director. But I think there is still another line you could excel in to even a greater extent, should you try."

Ruth, studying him intently, still failed to comprehend.

"Haven't you ever thought," the words came with a rush, "what a fine actress you would make?"

Ruth gasped, looked at the director of the Alectrion Film Corporation as though she thought he had gone mad.

"Me, an actress! Why, I never heard of such a thing!"

"You have faced the camera before," Mr. Hammond reminded her.

"Oh, I know! But not in a picture like this—not as a star working opposite an actor like Layton Boardman! I—I never—why, I couldn't!"

"I'm quite sure you could," asserted Mr. Hammond. Now that the thing had been proposed, he was smilingly confident. "And I am certain the idea will appeal to you, once you get used to it."

CHAPTER 17

RUTH DECIDES

As for Ruth, her head was whirling about in a fashion extremely unsettling to one of her usual composure and steady common sense.

She, act! A leading part! Such a notion had never entered her mind until Mr. Hammond abruptly put it there. It was flattering, this proposal of his, but the thing was utterly impossible.

She was saved the necessity of an immediate response by the arrival of Helen and Tom. The former was all exclamations and sympathy and flung herself upon Ruth at once with a flood of questions.

"That terrible Viola!" she cried, with a ferocious scowl. "You were right enough in suspecting her, Ruth. I only wish I had her here for a few minutes! And now what will you do for a leading woman?" and she regarded Ruth's flushed face with commiserating eyes.

"I've already suggested a remedy to Miss Ruth," said Mr. Hammond, trying to appear casual. "But, somehow or other, she doesn't appear to think much of it."

"A remedy?" repeated Tom, puzzled. "What possible remedy can there be? Unless," turning jocularly to Mr. Hammond, "you have brought an actress with you in your pocket."

"Perhaps I have merely found one up here," returned the older man, evidently enjoying the mystification of the two young people.

Ruth roused herself. Her face felt feverish and her hands were as cold as ice.

"Mr. Hammond suggests," she said, in a small voice, "that I play the lead myself. Oh, Tom, I don't know! What do you think?" and she fixed her gaze on the young man's face.

There was a moment of startled silence. It was Helen who broke into loud exclamations of approval.

"What a wonderful idea! Why, of course, you were just made to act, Ruth! I've watched you myself sometimes with that very thought in my mind. What an excellently simple solution!"

Ruth shook her head dubiously.

"I wish I thought so," she said. "But I've never seriously thought of acting. I've never wanted to, in fact. At least, not after the thrill of my part in 'The Heart of a Schoolgirl' passed," and the girl smiled slightly. "I've been too happy constructing vehicles for others and directing—"

"That's just it," Mr. Hammond broke in. "Any one who can direct others in as masterly a style as you can, Miss Ruth, ought certainly to be able to direct herself."

Ruth shook her head, eyes narrowed thoughtfully.

"I'm not a bit sure. I haven't much faith in my acting ability. Besides, we can't even tell whether or not I'll film well."

"That can soon be settled," said Mr. Hammond, waiving the objection aside. "Any one with your straight, regular features is almost bound to film well. And you've got the eyes—no doubt of that."

Ruth fell silent, thinking over Mr. Hammond's proposal, turning it over, looking at it from every angle. He had had a great deal of experience in the pictures, much more than she. He had picked a number of the present-day stars. Why was it not possible that his judgment was good in her case?

Helen chatted on excitedly over the prospect, occasionally exchanging views with Mr. Hammond. But Tom, despite Ruth's appeal to him, was silent, almost morose, and after a time Ruth noticed this silence.

She looked up at him, studying his thoughtful face for a moment. Then she touched his arm.

"You aren't crazy over the idea, are you, Tom?" she asked, her voice a bit wistful.

Tom looked startled. It was as though she had discovered some secret thought that he was trying to hide.

"I haven't had time to think of it yet," he answered evasively; but after a moment he turned to her on impulse: "Will you take a walk with me, Ruth? I'd like to talk to you."

Ruth turned to Mr. Hammond and Helen.

"Will you excuse us?" she said.

"Certainly," replied Mr. Hammond.

Helen, however, looked a little vexed.

"Now, Ruth Fielding, don't go off and let Tom Cameron persuade you not to do it!" she exclaimed. "I'm crazy to see you as a screen star!"

"A flickering little star, I'm afraid," responded Ruth dully, as she and Tom left the porch and turned toward Golden Pass.

They walked for some distance in silence, Tom morose, hands thrust deep in his pockets, Ruth busy with her own thoughts and willing that he should take the lead in the conversation.

Finally the young fellow kicked viciously at a stone in his path and vigorously voiced his protest.

"I don't know that I like this new wrinkle at all, Ruth!" he burst out.

"What new wrinkle?" queried Ruth, frowning.

"You know very well what I'm talking about. This suggestion of Mr. Hammond's that you take up acting."

Ruth was silent for a moment. Tom's tone hurt her. Perhaps he was as doubtful as she of her ability to act!

"I think myself that it's rather absurd," she said at last.

Tom stole a look at her face, then reached out suddenly and captured one of the brown hands that hung at her side.

"Oh, hang it all, Ruth, you know I don't mean that you can't act! I know you can—as I know you can do anything else that you want to, you wonderful girl!"

Ruth was sincerely puzzled, groping in the dark.

"Then, if it isn't that, what is it?" she demanded. "Why don't you want me to try this thing?" she persisted when he remained silent. "I'm desperate, Tom, as indeed you should be too. It seems to me we ought to welcome any chance that would help us to tide over this trouble. If by any chance we find that Mr. Hammond is right and that I can act acceptably, why shouldn't I? We'll save the salary of a leading woman, as well as this heart-breaking delay."

She looked so lovely to him in her earnestness that Tom's heart melted within him. He looked at her pleadingly.

"Can't you see what I mean—and make allowances for my feeling? If you take the feminine lead in your own picture you will have to play opposite Layton Boardman."

Of course she would have to play opposite Layton Boardman. But, for that matter, a great many well-known actresses would have been glad of the privilege.

"What earthly difference will it make?" she asked.

Tom groaned.

"No difference to you, I suppose," he said, thrusting his hands savagely into his pockets. "But maybe you think I am going to enjoy seeing that chap hold you in his arms as he has to do in the last scene?"

Ruth was given the vision to see how hard this would be for Tom, even though she could not sympathize with his jealousy.

"I'm sorry, Tom, but I can't see any other way out. After all, the whole thing is artificial, you know, just play-acting—Layton's lovemaking along with the rest. It's simply in the pictures."

It was lucky for both Ruth and Tom that the former did not understand nor ask him to repeat the sentence he muttered under his breath. "If I could be sure it was all just play acting!" was what he said, and there was no mistaking the doubt in his voice.

But Ruth did not hear. She was already busy with her plans.

"Anyway," she said, as they turned to retrace their steps to the house. "I haven't decided to do it yet, you know."

If Ruth had consulted her own feelings she would have taken several days to think over Mr. Hammond's suggestion. As it was, she felt that every day was precious, not only because of the salaries and other expenses piling up but because she feared the effect delay might have on the morale of her company. She had trained them and urged them to the "acting pitch" and she wanted to take full advantage of their enthusiasm.

Also, she knew Mr. Hammond could not stay at Golden Pass an unlimited amount of time and there was the fear at the back of her mind that, Mr. Hammond gone, she would never have the courage to follow his suggestion.

So it happened that on the second evening after his remarkable proposal a rather timid and embarrassed and altogether unusual Ruth approached Mr. Hammond as he stood in laughing conversation with Tom on the porch of the ranch house.

Both turned and saw at once the excitement that made Ruth's eyes dark and her cheeks unusually pink. Mr. Hammond put out a kindly hand to her.

"Going to do it?" he challenged.

"Yes!" whispered Ruth, and on the word that committed her something wonderful and breathtaking surged up within her, making her strong, confident and glad.

79

CHAPTER 18

A NEW ROLE

Ruth Fielding scarcely slept at all that night. Her thoughts went whirling round and round in an endless circle. She was not the least tired, only restless and eager.

On the morrow she was to face the camera in an all-important part—she, who had directed so many others just how to do it! They were to be test films only, to determine whether or not she would film well, whether or not her particular type of good looks would show well on the screen.

Ruth had studied her face long and attentively the evening before, studied it at every possible angle, impersonally, critically, as though it had been a perfectly strange face to her. As a matter of fact, it might almost have been a stranger's face from the number of surprising things Ruth found out about it. She had been too engrossed all through the years in her play and work to think much of her looks one way or another. Last night she had found out that Ruth Fielding's face was something more than a good practical face. It was, she had to admit it, even though she blushed in the dark over her lack of modesty, an unusually attractive and pleasing face. Some, she thought, still impersonally, might call it handsome.

It was a surprising, but extremely satisfying, discovery.

Having finished with her face, Ruth's thoughts veered to Tom and Helen and the different manner in which the two had accepted her decision the night before.

Helen had been delighted, enthusiastic, but, Ruth could not help feeling, a wee bit envious. For where is the girl, even one engaged and in love, who does not in her heart cherish an ambition to be a movie star? But on the whole Helen had been very satisfactory, had kissed her chum and hugged her and predicted great things for her future.

Tom had been different. This time he had not even attempted to hide his disapproval, his wretched jealousy, she thought resentfully. Had Mr. Hammond understood the reason for Tom's detached, glum mood? She wondered, and finally decided that he could not very well have helped doing so.

Well, defiantly, she would have to learn to go ahead and do as she thought best whether Tom approved or not. Why should she care, anyway?

But even at the moment she knew that she cared very, very much indeed what Tom thought.

"If he would only be sensible! If he would only behave himself!" she whispered to herself.

At this period Ruth fell asleep and awoke a scant two hours later to find the sun shining in the window.

Even then she did not feel tired. Her chief worry was lest she had overslept. She got up, looked at her wrist watch, and reached for her clothes all in the same instant.

A chuckle from the bed made her turn toward it. Helen was awake, regarding her with lazy, laughing eyes.

"Good morning, Star," said the young lady, adding whimsically: "How does it feel?"

Ruth went over and sat down on the side of the bed, putting a cold hand over Helen's warm one.

"I—I'm just scared to death!" she confessed.

"Looking as you do this morning," returned Helen, looking her chum over impartially and critically, "you have no earthly right to be scared of anything."

Ruth laughed and again reached for her clothes.

"You're a darling, Helen. But see that you stand by me today. I sort of feel I'll need all the backing I can get!"

But there were so many things for Ruth to decide, so many plans to make, that she forgot all about being selfconscious or frightened.

The tests were taken right after breakfast and it seemed as if everybody on the ranch turned out to see them. Even the cowboys were interested, sensing the dramatic possibilities of the event.

There was not one of them who did not like and admire Ruth personally and there were several who cherished even warmer emotions in regard to the charming author-director. That these emotions did not reach the stage of audible expression was due entirely to Ruth's manner. Pleasant, friendly, she always was, but beyond that she would not go—and no one else dared go.

Ruth went through the various tests with a skill and ease that amazed herself. She had not realized before how much she had learned of the difficult art of acting in her capacity as scenario writer and director. But what her modesty failed to point out to her was that she was a born actress as well. Before she had been posing five minutes every one on the lot but Ruth could see that.

Layton Boardman was there, watching Ruth with a queer expression in his narrowed eyes. No one could tell whether he was criticizing or admiring.

But when, the tests over, Ruth made her way through a throng of on-lookers, Layton Boardman stepped over to her and held out his hand.

"My congratulations," he said in a low tone, his gray eyes holding hers. "But—I am congratulating myself even more!"

For a moment Ruth could not draw her eyes from Boardman's. There was something heady, intoxicating in the actor's spontaneous praise. Then she realized that he was still holding her hand and drew it quickly away.

"You said that very nicely," she said lightly, to cover her confusion, and moved on.

Tom had not missed the little interchange. He was in a savage mood as he turned away from the ranch house and started toward the hills.

What was the use of adding his congratulations to the chorus of Ruth's admirers? he asked himself. She would miss neither him nor his praise. He thought of Boardman and clenched his hands. Time enough to get even with the fellow!

Meanwhile, Ruth was glad enough to escape to the comparative privacy of the ranch house. She had never felt so appallingly conspicuous in her life and, not being used to it, the experience rather staggered her.

Nevertheless she was excited, exalted, in a mood for almost anything to happen.

In the living room Helen flung her arms about her chum and kissed her.

"Ruthie, you were marvelous! Just think of all the time you have been wasting your talents!"

Ruth shook her head and pushed Helen gently from her.

"You are all combining to spoil me," she said. "What I need now is a clear head, if I ever had one in my life."

"I'll wager there's nothing the matter with your head, Miss Ruth," said Mr. Hammond, smiling genially down upon her. "I've never yet found anything wrong with it."

"There has to be a beginning to everything," Ruth reminded him gravely, and then they all laughed together, like excited and gleeful children. Though under Ruth's laughter was a little ache as she wondered where Tom was.

"But seriously," said Ruth, when their laughter had subsided, "I feel the need of good and well-seasoned advice—I feel it badly. What I want to know," she turned to Mr. Hammond, "is whether you know of any one I could get for a moderate salary to come down here and give me the points on acting my inexperience so badly needs. I know it is asking a good deal," she added anxiously, "but I do feel that I must have the advantage of some one else's experience."

"That was the very thing I intended to discuss with you," said Mr. Hammond. He drew up a chair close to the couch on which the two girls were sitting and fixed Ruth with an earnest eye. "I know the very woman for your purpose," he announced.

Ruth leaned forward, her eyes shining.

"I believe you must have Aladdin's lamp with you, Mr. Hammond," she said whimsically. "Every time you rub it a wish comes true."

"I wish that were always so," he responded, smiling. "But if I can make any wishes of yours come true, I'm very happy."

"About this woman you speak of," Ruth prompted eagerly. "Do I know her?"

"You undoubtedly have heard of her," Mr. Hammond responded. "Every one in the picture world has. She served during the World War with the Red Cross and was twice decorated for bravery—"

"Oh, I know," Ruth interrupted breathlessly. "You are speaking of Edith Lang, aren't you? And she was wounded in the leg while ministering to wounded soldiers behind the lines, wasn't she?"

Mr. Hammond nodded gravely.

"And you may recollect that later blood poisoning set in and she had to lose her leg."

Helen uttered an exclamation of pity.

"How terrible—and for an actress, too! What does she do now?"

"What she can," the man responded. "She can play a character part now and then—helpless invalids mostly where no action is required of her."

"Not very inspiring," said Ruth soberly.

"Exactly. And not very well paid either. But, for all that, Edith Lang is an excellent actress. Knows all the tricks of the trade and has a splendid thinking apparatus, as well."

"Do you suppose she would be willing to come out here to coach me in the tricks of the trade, as you say?" Ruth queried breathlessly.

"I happen to know," returned the other with decision, "that Edith Lang would be willing to do almost anything just now for the sake of steady occupation. She'd jump at the chance."

Ruth regarded her kind friend eagerly.

"Mr. Hammond, you are wonderful," she said. "You make me ashamed of my own stupidity. I will send for Edith Lang at once!"

CHAPTER 19

A NEW FRIEND

Ruth carried out her determination to send for Edith Lang, the crippled actress, immediately. She knew the reputation the screen star had enjoyed before her accident, and she felt, with Mr. Hammond, that Miss Lang was the very one to give her those points on acting which she felt were so necessary.

It was only a day or two after that that Ruth received an answering telegram in which Edith Lang announced that she was "on the way."

This welcome news, coupled with the information that the camera tests of herself had been a great success and that she filmed unusually well, served to encourage Ruth immensely. Had Tom only been more sympathetic she felt she would have been perfectly happy in spite of the heavy cost of the delay that Viola's defection caused.

Edith Lang appeared promptly on the dot and was met at the station by the rickety car—of which, by the way, Headwaters Ranch was inordinately proud.

Ruth's whole company turned out to meet the crippled actress on her arrival at the ranch, eager to give a cordial welcome to a gifted but unfortunate fellow artist.

When the car rattled up the drive and Edith Lang descended, those who waited to welcome her were surprised to see how easily she carried herself. They had expected to see some one on crutches.

But Edith Lang walked on two feet, and though one of them was artificial the only thing that attested to the fact was an almost imperceptible limp and a certain stiffness in her movements.

What they did not know was that only pride kept Edith Lang from hobbling painfully and that there were times when what was left of her leg pained so torturingly that not even pride could keep her on her feet.

She had been a beautiful woman, and was pretty still, although suffering had etched lines about her eyes and mouth and given her a slightly pinched, old look.

She smiled upon Ruth, though her face was white with the fatigue of the journey.

"I am Ruth Fielding," said the girl, as she slipped an arm within the older woman's and led her authoritatively toward the house. "My people have turned out in force to meet you, but we are going to save all introductions until later when you have rested."

"How kind you are, my dear—and attractive," said Edith Lang, with a searching glance into Ruth's flushed face. "I have heard much of you. You are justly famous. I have seen your picture, 'Snowblind.' It is perfect."

All this, while Ruth led her guest into the big front room of the ranch house and settled her in the most comfortable chair it contained.

This praise of *Snowblind* from so real an authority was sweet indeed to Ruth. She felt tremendously drawn to Edith Lang.

Helen had been hovering around in the background and now Ruth drew her forward and presented her to the newcomer.

"My very best friend," was Ruth's laughing introduction. "And soon to be married. Meaning, of course, the end of our good times together!"

Miss Lang smiled as she took off her hat and smoothed up her bright hair.

"Marriage means the end—and the beginning of many things," she said. Before she could continue Mr. Hammond came into the room, hand outstretched in cordial greeting.

The two were good friends, as was attested by their manner toward each other. Mr. Hammond settled down immediately for what he termed "a good old chat." But Ruth, seeing how very tired the newcomer looked, interposed firmly with the dictum that Miss Lang must have food and rest before being interviewed on any matter whatsoever.

Although the actress laughingly protested, Ruth could see that she was secretly relieved.

In the room assigned to her—the room deserted by Viola and now divested of every reminder of her, the trunks, various hat boxes and other luggage having been sent for and carried away—Miss Lang slipped into a pretty blue dressing gown and lay down upon the bed while Ruth drew the shades partly down to shut out the glare of the afternoon sun.

When the girl went over to the bed to see if there was anything more she could do for her crippled guest, Edith Lang caught the girl's hand in her own and smiled up at her.

"You are a dear girl," she said, "and very considerate of one—less fortunate." She closed her eyes for a moment, then opened them again to look at Ruth with an expression of lively interest.

"I have been studying you," she announced, "and I want to say, my dear, that I hardly need see you act to tell that you can. Besides good looks and a pretty figure, you have brains, which, as you very well know, are at a premium among our beautiful stars of the day. In fact," with a warm pressure of Ruth's hand, "I believe I am going to enjoy my new work thoroughly!"

Ruth left Edith Lang's presence, encouraged and inspired. Besides the pleasant things that had been said to her, Ruth felt that she had found a genuine friend in the actress.

Nor was this belief weakened in the busy days that followed. The friendship between Ruth and Miss Lang grew and strengthened while the work of picture-making went ahead with marvelous rapidity.

Having written the story and created her heroine, Ruth could throw herself into the part with more fervor and realism than would be possible for any one else. While she was acting, Ruth was not Ruth Fielding, but Ann Marks, suffering with the girl, fighting for her love, as the heroine fought. But in spite of this ability to lose herself in the part of the heroine, Ruth was honest enough to confess to herself that the criticism and guidance of Edith Lang were invaluable.

There were times when she felt awkward and embarrassed, was not quite sure how to carry her hands or where to place her feet.

At such times Edith Lang would call to her:

"You have an apron on, Miss Fielding. Remember, you are a little mountain girl, nervous and excited. Twist the corners of the apron—not too much —just enough to register mental distress. That's right—great, my dear. Face the camera more directly. Remember you must get your emotions across to the public. Fine!"

Or, at another time:

"You have just heard that your lover has been wounded by the outlaws, perhaps fatally. You forget yourself utterly in your despair. Can you cry? Good! Oh, my dear, that is wonderful! You have art. Now your lover suddenly appears. He is wounded, but not fatally. You run to him, smiling through your tears. Do not keep your back turned too long—remember your back tells little—turn toward the camera—closer, closer—"

And so on from day to day, until Ruth, becoming experienced in her turn, came to know instinctively what was the right thing to do.

"But I never could have done anything without you," she told Miss Lang gratefully one day. "There are so many things to learn!"

Miss Lang patted her hand, laughing.

"You are an apt pupil, my dear, and one it is a pleasure to teach," she said.

Finally all the smaller scenes were shot. It remained then to make arrangements for the big moment in her picture—the avalanche.

Mr. Hammond had lingered on long past his intention, fascinated by Ruth's work in her new rôle. He accompanied her each day to location, watched her, and, with Miss Lang, advised and criticized where criticism was needed.

Ruth, in love with her new work, drank in these criticisms eagerly and profited by them so quickly that both her critics were delighted.

Meanwhile, Tom had an amusing little adventure all his own—at least, it would have been amusing if he could have kept it to himself.

It all happened in the first place because he was worried about Ruth. She was doing some pretty dangerous acts in company with "that Boardman chap." In spite of Tom's respect for the westerner's prowess on horseback, he had not reached the point where he could watch with any degree of calm a scene in which the actor was supposed to swoop Ruth up before him on his horse and race with her at thrilling speed along a narrow ledge where a single swerve or misstep would mean almost certain disaster.

Tom had pleaded with Ruth to let some one double for her in this scene. But the girl was now thoroughly interested in her rôle and would not hear to following his suggestion.

"They would all think I was afraid," Ruth pointed out to him. "Besides, there isn't the slightest danger, Tommy."

Since Tom could not agree with her on this point he decided to take a tramp into the hills while this scene was being shot.

"I can't keep her from risking her life if she wants to," he told himself as he shouldered his rifle and started afoot along the narrow, rocky trail. "But I don't have to stay and watch the awful deed."

Tom knew in a general way whither he was bound. The spot had been a favorite of his from the moment he had discovered it—a great bare rock that jutted out above Golden Pass and commanded an awe-inspiring view of mountains and ravines beyond.

However, Tom found that the gorgeous view only reminded him the more of Ruth and the perilous scene she was to take part in.

So he deserted the rock and made his way into the shadowy woods, there to wander and explore until it should be time again to return to the ranch.

The mysterious sights and sounds of the forest fascinated him, drew him farther and farther into the heart of it until he came to a narrow little path, trampled hard by the feet of countless denizens of the forest.

"Bet this leads to a water hole," Tom said to himself. "Wish Ruth was with me—she never gets time off from her acting to enjoy herself any more."

He kept on along the path and presently saw the glimmer of water through the trees.

"The old water hole," he told himself triumphantly, and the next moment stepped out upon the edge of it. As he did so something rose from the farther bank and slipped quietly and stealthily into the woods.

"It was a deer, I bet," Tom muttered. A gleam came into his eyes and he raised his gun, only to lower it again despondently. "Closed season," he warned himself. "Anyway, it might be any sort of animal. I didn't get a real look at it."

The spot was picturesque in the extreme and Tom thought that if he stayed around for a while and made himself seem only a part of the scenery he might see something interesting. Judging from the hard ground of the path, many wild creatures must frequent this mountain pool. Tom thought, with a grin, that it would be fun to watch these denizens of the woodland when they did not know themselves observed.

He found a splendid post of observation—a large flat rock backed by a tree against which he might rest weary shoulders if he wished.

Tom settled himself comfortably and waited.

For a long time nothing stirred about the pool. Evidently the woodland folk were still a bit uneasy about the presence of a man creature. However, as Tom remained very still they gained confidence and one by one stole through the heavy underbrush to drink hastily, cast a wary glance in Tom's direction and scuttle back to the safety of the woods. Once a fox made its appearance and Tom's fingers tightened instinctively on his rifle where it lay at his side upon the rock.

However, no other movement betrayed his presence and the fox appeared to take no notice of him. It drank lazily, insolently, then turned away and disappeared in the direction from which it had come.

"What a fine neck-piece you'd make for some one, old boy," Tom mused. "Just the same, your coat will be thicker and finer when the winter comes."

Wearied by his cramped position, Tom was about to get up when a noise in the woods behind him caused him to change his mind.

Something was crashing heavily through the underbrush—beast or man, Tom could not tell which. But he sat very still, fingers coiled about his rifle.

CHAPTER 20

NOT ACTING

The next moment Tom felt an uncomfortable chill creep along his spine. His jumping nerves commanded action, but his common sense said, "Don't move!"

Breaking through the underbrush not six feet from where he sat rigid upon the rock, blundered the largest, brownest and most dangerous looking bear Tom Cameron had ever seen!

Lightning thoughts raced through Tom's head. This was not his first experience with bears, and he felt that this one might not attack him unless he himself showed fight. Even in that case, the bear would probably rather retreat than advance. Almost instantly Tom made his decision. He would stay where he was, as motionless as possible, and trust to the chance that the bear would not observe him.

It took bravery, not so much to make the decision, as to act upon it. Tom's instinct was to jump to his feet, seize his rifle and give battle, counting on the element of surprise to vanquish his enemy. It required every ounce of self-control he possessed to force himself to sit still and watch that bear.

Evidently the animal had not yet discovered the presence of his enemy. The wind, luckily, was blowing away from Tom. Then, too, it soon became apparent that the bear was in playful mood. Startled as he was, Tom had an impulse to laugh at the absurd antics of the huge creature.

It waddled off first to the borders of the pool where it studied its reflection as intently as any pretty girl might have done.

Afterward it posed, cocking its head to one side and raising a clumsy, vicious-nailed paw.

"One blow from that—" thought Tom and cut the thought off short. He watched the movements of the beast with fascinated attention.

But the bear still took no notice of him. Slipping off the bank into the shallow water, it bathed and wallowed luxuriously, ducking its head under water and puffing for all the world like some fat man short of breath.

His toilette completed, he lumbered up upon the bank again and rolled over on the soft moss.

"That's his bath towel," thought Tom, still in a detached way as though he were a spectator at a play, safely established in an orchestra seat. "Whew, he's bound to see me now!"

However, bruin either did not see the man sitting so motionless on the rock or he chose to ignore him. But after rolling about on the ground for some time, he got up and started directly toward Tom!

Again the young fellow felt the tingling along his spine, again his fingers closed about the barrel of his gun.

But the bear wore an amiable, benignant expression. He waddled clumsily forward and lay down on the farther end of Tom's rock!

It was a huge rock, to be sure, and several feet still separated the young man from the bear, but to Tom's excited fancy that rock was becoming altogether too crowded for comfort!

Gently his fingers lifted the gun, stealthily and slowly he started to slip off his end of the rock. Suddenly every nerve cried out and he sprang to his feet with a jerk.

A voice had reached him, a familiar voice.

"Tom! Oh, Tom! where are you?"

At the same time bruin sat up, blinking sleepily. Tom saw Ruth coming toward him through the trees, but was too late to signal her to retreat.

"I've had a fine time finding you!" she cried, reaching his side. Then, turning slowly to follow the direction of his rigid glance, "Tom! what *have* you got here—"

The words died in her throat as the bear, disturbed at this intrusion, muttered fretfully and took a step toward them.

"Stand still," Tom commanded in a whisper. "He doesn't want to fight."

If Tom had raised his gun then the temper of the animal would have changed. As it was, the steady stare of two pairs of human eyes bewildered him. He muttered fretfully deep down in his throat and, turning, ambled sullenly off into the woods.

"Since when," demanded Ruth unsteadily, as the crashing noise of the bear's retreat died off in the distance, "did you turn bear-trainer, Tom?"

But Tom was not inclined to laugh just then. With Ruth sharing his danger, the woods all at once seemed dark and sinister.

"Let's get out of this," he muttered. When they reached the sunlit trail again, they laughed together, however, as Tom recounted his queer experience and imitated the antics of the coquettish bear.

"Poor old thing," she said drolly. "He was just out for a nice bath and a nap and you spoiled it all. Wish we could have taken a picture of it," she said, with professional regret.

"Which reminds me," said Tom, "to ask how you happened to find your way into that deep, dark heart of the woods."

"I was looking for you," the girl admitted. "I wanted to consult you about some details for the avalanche. Some one said you had come up this way, so I followed you."

"That's a dangerous thing to do, Ruth," said Tom anxiously. "This isn't a zoölogical park, you know, with the wild animals caged up."

"I'm perfectly safe," said Ruth, patting the neat little revolver that hung at her belt. "You forget that, for the present at least, I am a cowgirl, Tom!"

CHAPTER 21

THE NARROW LEDGE

Little was discussed in the days that followed but the avalanche.

It was to be a tremendous spectacle and a great deal of preparation was necessary to insure an artistic filming of it.

Ruth and Tom had found what they considered an ideal location—a mountain, rising almost perpendicularly skyward, and at its base a few squat, rambling little cabins.

Ruth had been forced to pay a ridiculously high sum for these cabins. But Tom and she figured that to erect others, no matter how flimsily built, would cost even more. Fortunately, not all the cabins were occupied. Had they been, the Fielding Film Company never could have afforded the price. Some had been deserted long since and were falling to pieces. As Helen laughingly declared, it would be "a mercy to put them out of the way."

In the picture, bandits were supposed to descend upon the little mining town, robbing, pillaging, and, after a strenuous fight, capturing the heroine, Ann Marks, and her handsome cowboy lover.

After binding the pair securely, the bandits, alarmed at the sound of pursuit, were to fling their victims into one of the deserted cabins and make off.

As they dash about the side of the mountain the avalanche, tons of dirt and rock from the mountainside, overtakes them, burying them beneath its weight and wrecking most of the cabins.

Of course the bandits are to be engulfed by the landslide while the cabin in which the lovers were imprisoned would miraculously escape the full force of the avalanche. Though partly buried beneath débris, the roof of the cabin holds and the hero and heroine, severing their bonds, are at last able to struggle through to sunlight and safety.

Of course Ruth and Boardman were not to remain in the cabin during the avalanche. These, as well as Tom and the rest of the company who were to be imperiled by the landslide, had planned to take refuge in a cave at the foot of the mountain. This cave was so situated that it would escape the débris of the avalanche.

Then one day, when everything was almost ready, Ruth had an accident that came near to putting her out of the reckoning entirely.

She and Helen, with Boardman and Tom, had climbed halfway up the mountainside to inspect the little shack where the dynamite was stored and to give last minute directions for the preparation of the landslide.

"All the dynamite that isn't used for the avalanche must be removed as far as possible from the scene before the landslide takes place," Ruth observed.

"I've already given orders to that effect," Tom assured her, and the girl squeezed his arm affectionately. Dear old Tom, always so dependable.

Then it was that Ruth, in an impulsive moment, precipitated disaster upon herself.

She stepped out upon the little ledge of rock and soft dirt from which one might stare down at the precipitous slope of the mountain.

They had come by a circuitous route, a little path that wound snakelike, clinging close to the mountainside. But at this point, rocky and menacing, the mountain seemed to forbid descent.

"I wonder if any one could get down from here," she said curiously. "I declare, I'd like to try!"

At the moment the soft earth crumbled treacherously from beneath her feet! Ruth flung herself backward—but too late. Before any one could reach her, Ruth was gone—had disappeared completely over the lip of the ledge.

Tom sprang forward, flung out his arm to catch the girl. But the whole thing, the terrible, incredible thing, happened so swiftly that he missed his grip and felt only her dress slide tantalizingly through his fingers.

Now, grim-lipped, he knelt and peered over the ledge.

Behind him Helen, terror-stricken, was wailing:

"Ruth! Ruth! She'll be killed on those rocks!"

"Keep still!" Tom commanded roughly. He looked up to see Boardman at his side. It needed only a glance to tell him that Boardman had seen also.

Ruth hung there, not ten feet below, grasping the slight trunk of a sapling, feeling for a foothold with her feet on the smooth, treacherous rock.

Tom's mind worked quickly. Only a few feet below Ruth was a ledge of rock. It was only about two feet wide; still it was enough, provided one jumping from a height of fifteen feet could judge the distance accurately and keep his balance once he landed.

"Hold fast!" he called to Ruth, praying that she would have strength to hold her weight until he could get to her. "It's all right, girl. Catch hold with your other hand. I'm coming down."

Layton Boardman, behind him, had seen what Tom was about about to do and was protesting.

"It's a crazy stunt! You'll kill yourself, man!"

Tom gave him a look.

"Maybe," he said briefly. "Meanwhile, go for a rope. Get help here as quickly as you can. Hurry."

Boardman stopped no more to argue. There was something in Tom's tone that compelled obedience.

He turned and ran down the trail they had traversed only a short time before. Helen, clinging to a tree, shaking, white, called to Tom.

"If I can do anything——"

"You can pray," said Tom softly, and let himself over the lip of the ledge.

Ruth was still clinging to the tree, gazing up at him, wide-eyed, terrified.

"Tom, don't do it! You will kill yourself! I'm all right! I can hold on till some one gets a rope. Tom! Go back! Go back!"

"Save your strength, Ruth. I'm coming."

With a prayer in his heart, Tom lowered himself till he hung only by his fingers to the treacherous ledge. There was a tree, a sapling like that to which Ruth clung, close to that ledge fifteen feet below. Would he be able to grasp that? Upon that possibility, he knew, his fate hung, and Ruth's as well.

The girl could never sustain her weight until Boardman returned with a rope and help. Her fingers would become numb, gradually slip their hold——

Tom allowed himself no further time for reflection. Swinging his body away from the cliff, he let go his hold, felt himself dropping! Would he reach the ledge? Could he keep his balance?

The sharp edges of rocks, of rough earth, tore at him, raking his hands and face, but he scarcely felt them.

Down, down, and then a jarring thump that made him reel dizzily backward. With all the force of his body he flung himself forward and reached out desperately.

The tree—the tree—his feet were slipping—he had it—the blessed feel of the rough bark under his fingers!

Tom drew himself against the face of the cliff and clung there for a moment to regain his breath.

The worst, the hardest part, was still to come. And it must come soon, he knew that.

Even in the moment that he rested, Ruth's voice called down to him.

"Tom! Tom, are you all right?"

"All right, dear. Can you hold on a minute more?"

"I—I guess so," Ruth's voice was not so confident as it had been. "My fingers—I'm afraid I'm losing my grip."

"All right! Now listen carefully and I'll tell you what to do. I'm right beneath you, Ruth. See—I can touch your foot. Rest it a moment in my hand—that's the girl! Now, when you drop, keep close to the side of the cliff. Let yourself go. I'll catch you."

"Let go! Oh, Tom, I can't!" Ruth's voice sounded breathless, faint. "That terrible drop!"

"You've got to do it, Ruth. There's no other way. I'll catch you."

"All right!" came valiantly and in a louder tone. "Are you ready?"

"Ready!" replied Tom, and braced himself.

CHAPTER 22

A TEST OF COURAGE

It was an extreme test of courage to do what Ruth Fielding did then. To let oneself go blindly, trusting to another's strength and skill to save one from a terrible death, takes bravery of the highest.

Perhaps if any one but Tom had been waiting for her there below Ruth could not have done what she did. But it was Tom—Tom, who, she knew, would give his life for her, who was always there when she needed him.

Without daring to let herself think longer Ruth unwound her numbed fingers from about the trunk of the tree and let herself drop.

Tom saw her coming, leaned outward, caught her as she fell. For a moment they swung out above that dizzy depth, only the strength of Tom's arm between them and disaster.

Ruth did her best, throwing her weight forward, scrambling for a foothold on the ledge. By a superhuman effort Tom regained his balance and his sure foothold on the ledge. He drew Ruth to him, holding her reassuringly.

"We're all right, now," he said huskily in her ear. "That was luck."

"Not luck!" panted Ruth. She was feeling faint and sick with the reaction and it was only by a tremendous effort that she kept herself upright, even with the strength of Tom's arm about her. "It wasn't luck," she managed to say. "It was just plain pluck, Tommy-boy. No one else would have thought of doing what you did."

Something in the tone of the girl's voice caused Tom to look at her sharply.

"Do you feel sick?" he asked, for her face was ashen white.

Ruth managed a smile through tight lips.

"A little dizzy," she admitted. "I don't dare look down or up."

"Don't, then. Shut your eyes."

Ruth shook her head.

"That only makes it ten times worse." Then in a minute as she saw him looking anxiously at her, she added: "I'm all right, Tom. Don't worry about me."

Tom replied cheerfully that he was not worried—that he could bet on her always.

But in his heart he was anxious enough. The pallor of Ruth's face was enough to show her condition. If she should faint there on that narrow ledge of rock how long could he hold her with only the sapling to cling to, and his left hand at that?

Well, he decided grimly, if worst came to worst, they would go together —that was some comfort.

He cast an anxious glance aloft. Boardman should be back by this time. It seemed ages that they had been clinging there.

Tom felt Ruth sag against him and looked down at her again. She was fighting with all her strength the waves of nausea and faintness that threatened to engulf her.

"Hold on, Ruth, just a minute or two more. Boardman's sure to get here soon."

He looked up again and saw Helen peering over at them. She was lying prone on the ground, afraid otherwise to approach that perilous ledge.

"They're coming!" she cried to Tom's questioning, upturned face. "I can hear them coming up the trail. Can you hold on, Tommy-boy?"

"Sure!" Tom's voice was hopeful, even buoyant. "Did you hear what she said?" he added to the half-fainting girl at his side. "They'll be here in a jiffy now."

Ruth lifted her head and tried to smile.

"Good!" was all she said, but Tom knew that there was plenty of the fighting spirit left in her yet.

It was a matter of only a few minutes before they heard excited voices overhead, Helen's quick answers, Boardman's curt commands.

Looking up, Tom saw that the actor held a lariat in his hands and was twirling it with practiced skill. The next moment a loop of rope descended and settled gently about Ruth's shoulders.

"Under your arms, Ruth. Here, I'll help," cried Tom.

Between them they managed to get the loop of the rope beneath Ruth's arms.

"All right?" called Boardman.

"All right!" responded Tom, and the actor drew taut the noose, fitting the rope snugly.

A dozen hands added their strength to Boardman's, and in a moment Ruth felt herself drawn over the edge of the precipice—found her feet once more on solid ground.

"Tom!" she stammered, as Helen's arms went eagerly about her.

"He's all right. We'll get him next," promised Boardman.

A moment more and Tom was standing, shaken but smiling, among them while a dozen admiring cowboys shook him by the hand or pounded him on the back in admiration of his nerve.

"You sure was flirtin' with the undertaker that time, mister," one of them remarked, as Tom, feeling very sheepish and not in the least like the hero they were trying to make of him, pushed himself through the group to where Helen was standing with her arm about Ruth.

"Feeling better?" he asked the latter.

"Ever so much!" she responded, but Tom saw that she was still fighting nausea and faintness. Without a word he caught Ruth up in his arms and strode with her down the mountain trail.

A short distance within the woods they found horses tethered to the trees, evidently the mounts of the cowboys who had ridden with Layton Boardman to the rescue.

Tom, unasking, appropriated one of these, placed Ruth in the saddle, and swung himself up behind her.

"It isn't Layton Boardman this time," he could not resist saying as Ruth rested contentedly against his big shoulder.

"You were wonderful, Tom!" she said. "I'll never forget what you did—never!"

All Headwaters Ranch was roused by Ruth's accident and Tom's spectacular method of rescue. Every one visited the spot, examined the tiny ledge, and wondered how any one could drop to it and retain his balance. Each one was quite sure he could not have performed the feat. Needless to say, Tom's heroism raised him immensely in the estimation of every one. As for Ruth, she never approached that spot again without a reminiscent shudder.

The girl had scant opportunity to dwell on her narrow escape, however, for as the day approached for the staging of the avalanche innumerable details had to be attended to, the scene rehearsed again and again.

At last everything was in readiness—dynamite had been planted, extras well instructed. Tomorrow the scene would be taken—the great, the climactic scene of the whole drama. Every one was on edge, excited, keyed to a high nervous tension.

Tom, knowing the inevitable danger to the actors in a thing of the sort, went around with an anxious frown on his brow, at times stopping to exhort Ruth to be careful.

"Of course I'll be careful, Tom," she said impatiently at last. "But, really, it's foolish of you to worry so. There isn't a mite of actual danger."

"Just the same," he told her, "I'll be pretty thankful when tomorrow is safely over."

Tomorrow came and with it the promise of another fine, sunshiny day. Ruth's entire company was on tiptoe with expectation.

As soon as possible after breakfast Ruth ordered the company out on location. They went gladly, excitedly, catching something of Ruth's intense enthusiasm, resolved to back up their "leading lady" to the limit.

It was a great party that started into the mountains that sparkling morning. Miss Lang rode in state in the ranch flivver. Mr. Hammond, who had prolonged his stay out of all reason, cantered gallantly at her side.

On horseback, Ruth, with Helen and Tom on either side of her, led the rest of her company, including the cameramen, while in the rear a veritable army of cowboys—those to be used as extras in the scene and others who came along merely out of curiosity—zipped and hurrahed along the dusty road.

Upon reaching location it took but a short time for the cameramen to set their cameras in position and the company to get ready for spirited action.

"I have a feeling," said Ruth to Boardman, as she spurred her horse toward the group of cabins at the foot of the mountain, "that something tremendous is going to happen this morning—a picture that will give points to the best one I ever made!"

Layton Boardman smiled.

"It's in the air!" he agreed, and galloped after her.

At the word of command from the film director, the little band of desperate bandits descended upon the unsuspecting mining town and cameras started to grind busily. The "big doings" were on!

Everything went exactly as it had been planned and the fight before the cabins was spirited and realistic. Then the great moment was at hand! A close-up had been taken of Ruth and Boardman bound hand and foot in the deserted cabin. The next moment—the camera having finished with them—they had slipped their bonds and were dashing with the rest of Ruth's company toward the safety of the mountain cave.

The time for the avalanche was at hand!

CHAPTER 23

BURIED ALIVE

Tom had accompanied Shepley, to help him direct the scene of the fight with the bandits. Tom's advice on fighting tactics was always worth listening to and Shepley was glad of any assistance he might give in handling the extras. There was another point to be gained—and this was quite a personal one with Tom—he would be with Ruth during the course of the avalanche.

Now he seized her arm and half-carried, half-pushed her into the cave. The place was pretty well filled when they got there and Ruth was more than ever glad that the cave was a large one.

There was a moment of tense excitement. One of the boys put his hands over his ears as though to shut out the expected sound of exploding dynamite.

Ruth tucked her hand within Tom's arm. The boy put his big one over it, holding her fingers firmly.

"Aren't you glad I'm here?" he whispered. "Honest?"

"Honest, I am," she whispered in return.

The next moment it came—what they had been waiting for with held breath. A sharp explosion, and the rumble and roar of dislodged rock and dirt starting on its downward slide.

"Here it comes!"

"Oh boy, I wish we were out there with the cameramen to watch it!" some one yelled.

Then, suddenly, cutting off the exclamations of those within the cave, came a second explosion, so loud, so deafening, that the first might have been the popping of a child's toy pistol.

It seemed as though the whole mountain shook, rocked on its base. There was a rending, tearing, grinding sound as tons of the dislodged mountainside swept downward to the valley.

All those in the cave backed instinctively away from the opening. It was well that they did, for at the moment, the light of day was shut out for them, tons of rock and dirt piling up before the mouth of the cave, barring their way to freedom!

It was a second or more before the extent of the calamity appeared to them.

It was Ruth who spoke first, her voice sounding faint and eerie in that intense gloom.

"Tom, do you realize? We're buried alive in here! What do you suppose happened? That second explosion—"

"Wasn't in the picture at all," Tom finished grimly. "Don't you suppose I know it?"

"Then what—"

"The dynamite house," Tom explained briefly. "I told them to take it all away—what we didn't need of the dynamite. The fools evidently forgot—"

"And we pay for it, mister," drawled one of the boys from the dark. "Looks like we'd been buried good and proper without any expenses of the funeral."

"Easy there!" Layton Boardman's voice came cool and grim. "Remember, if we're in jeopardy here, our part from now on is to work hard and say little."

"Do you think there's a chance to tunnel our way out?" Ruth asked eagerly.

"We can try. And it's safe to say that those outside won't sit around and twiddle their thumbs. Don't worry, Miss Fielding. We'll get out some way."

Tom could not but admire Boardman's poise and cool courage. What he said sounded almost convincing, but Tom knew that in his heart Boardman, like himself, had little hope of escape for any of them.

Blocked as their retreat was by tons of débris, how could they hope to dig a way out from within with only their bare hands for tools?

On the other hand, even though those on the outside who had witnessed the catastrophe set to work at once with all energy—as of course they would do—the chances were that they would not be able to burrow a way into the cave in time to save the company from smothering to death in those close quarters. Even now the air was getting hot, devitalized.

While Layton Boardman, some of the boys, and even Ruth, set to work at the gigantic task of tunneling a way to the outer air, Tom worked his way silently and unnoticed to the rear of the cave. He had no idea what he would find there—if indeed he found anything save the blank damp wall of dirt in which it had seemed to terminate. But, after all, exploration seemed worth while, the chance no more forlorn than that the others were taking.

He groped his way through the blackness. At last his fingers touched the earthy wall at the rear of the cave.

He felt his way cautiously along this and came at last to a spot where the earth wall seemed to end.

His breath caught in his throat. Was the rear of the cave not a solid wall then? Was this break a possible entrance to a second cave or a tunnel that they had not observed before?

He felt in his pocket for matches, found a box and cautiously struck one, shielding its flame with his hand. It was a moment before his eyes could make out anything beyond the tiny flickering light of the match. Then he uttered a low exclamation.

There was a break, an opening through which, by ducking his head, he could go.

The match was burning his fingers. Tom dropped it and cautiously entered the tunnel, progressing by the sense of touch. He did not strike another match for fear those in the main body of the cave might discover what he was about and convey the knowledge to Ruth. He had a horror of giving her false hope. This tunnel might lead anywhere or nowhere. It seemed, just now, to be leading directly into the heart of the mountain.

He groped his way along, carefully testing the walls of the tunnel on both sides of him for any sign of another opening.

But there was none. The walls of the passage presented a blank damp surface, and as Tom progressed he felt certain that these walls were closing in on him.

He was coming to the end probably, a converging of the tunnel into the solid wall of the mountainside, which meant defeat and hopelessness.

Tom's heart sank. A great horror rose in him. Not until that moment did he realize how much he had hoped for from this unexpected tunnel. With the snuffing out of that hope went his last shred of cheerfulness.

Buried alive! Shut in the horror and blackness of that cave! Such an end—and for Ruth!

What was that! Tom's hand, groping against the narrowing walls of the tunnel, suddenly slipped off into emptiness!

No wall there! Another break! Perhaps another tunnel!

Tom lighted a second match, and with trembling fingers held it aloft, shielded its feeble flame, peered, half in hope and half in dread, into the shadows beyond the light.

There was a break—another tunnel branching off into darkness. Tom lighted another match and advanced toward the opening. The flame flickered and went out, a curious thing in that airless place.

Swift hope rushed up in him. He stood a moment collecting himself, striving to think calmly.

There must be a current of air in that stifling place, otherwise the match would not have gone out! And a current of air meant only one thing—that there must be another exit from the cave, another opening into the outer air.

Not daring to let himself hope too much, Tom went forward and around the break in the tunnel wall, inch by inch, feeling his way.

Suddenly he stopped, head up. Before him, dim and far away, but undeniably there, gleamed a tiny ray of light.

With a hoarse cry Tom turned and stumbled back the way he had come. "Light! I see daylight!" he cried.

CHAPTER 24

BEARS

Meanwhile, those outside the cave had been witnesses to an unbelievable horror. There was the muttering, rending sound of the avalanche, earth torn from the breast of the mountain, a magnificent spectacle as tons of débris roared earthward, demolishing the cabins at the mountain's foot. Then, hard upon that first great rush of earth, a second explosion—an explosion that seemed to shake the mountain from towering tip to base, that tore up tortured earth and rock, a roar that drowned all other sounds in its immensity.

Then, silence—breathless, tense.

"The cave!" shrieked Helen. "It is gone! The mouth of it is gone!"

She flung herself into the arms of Edith Lang. The two clung together wordlessly. They watched while cowboys set feverishly to the task of excavation, using whatever tools came to hand. Others dashed back to the ranch for picks and shovels and reinforcements.

Mr. Hammond flung off his coat and joined those working at the pile of earth and rock. Commanding, suggesting, urging, he seemed to be everywhere at once.

Finally Helen roused herself from her numbed silence.

"They will never be able to get to them in time," she said hopelessly. "Why, it looks as if they would have to dig their way through the whole mountainside. Tom! Ruth! Oh, what shall I do!"

She rose with some wild idea in her head of adding her puny efforts to those of the rescuers.

Edith Lang guessed at her intention and gently pulled the girl down beside her again.

"You would only get in the way, dear. They are doing all they can."

"But it isn't enough!" Helen's hands were clenched. All color had left her face. "They will never get to them in time. Never—never!"

Her desperate cry was duplicated heartbreakingly by those within the cave. Although they knew that those on the outside must have come at once to the rescue, must be feverishly at work, even now, no sound of pick or shovel penetrated to their gloomy prison.

This fact in itself was enough to rob them of all hope. Had their rescue been possible, the voices and shouts of encouragement would be audible now.

They had dug at the imprisoning mass of rock and dirt until fingers were sore and bleeding. Some had found sharp stones and rocks and had continued the frantic digging with these poor implements.

Ruth realized suddenly how futile, how foolish, all their efforts were.

With a little cry of weariness and despair she straightened up and felt about for Tom. Not finding him, she became frightened. It was natural to suppose he had been at her side all this time.

She raised her voice and called his name aloud, at first faintly, then wildly, frantically.

"Tom, where are you? Tom!"

"Coming!"

There was an exultation, a wild gladness in that answering shout that thrilled and startled the prisoners in the cave. They got up from hands and knees, nursed bleeding fingers and peered with an intense, terrible hopefulness in the direction of Tom's voice.

"Ruth, where are you? Ruth!"

"Here, Tom!" she stretched out her hands to him, clinging to him. "Tom, what is it?"

"I've found another entrance to this place! There are tunnels, and at the far end is light—daylight. Do you hear that? Daylight!" His voice was husky and cracked and the shout that went up from a dozen answering throats was wild and hoarse with hope.

"Follow me!" Tom was already turning back toward the tunnel, his arm about Ruth. "You will have to go single file for the passage is narrow. Keep close behind me, Ruth. Hold to my coat."

Ruth held on to his coat. It is doubtful if anything on earth would have made her let go of it just then!

The whole company straggled after their leader, a weary, battered but hopeful group, yet not daring to hope too much.

Tom led them along the first passage then turned into the second.

There he paused, drew Ruth close to him, and pointed.

"Do you see it—the opening?" he asked.

Ruth, eyes upon that narrow ray of light, drew a sharp breath.

"Yes, I see it, Tom."

They said no more, for that much was eloquent, and Tom led the way again, going more cautiously now since the farther end of the passage had not yet been explored.

Their progress was slowed considerably by the fact that at this point the tunnel narrowed so sharply that they were forced to rub shoulders with the wall on either side.

At last they were reduced to proceeding crab fashion—going sideways and feeling their way, inch by inch.

Then, when they least expected it, the passage widened suddenly, forming a cave not dissimilar in size, it seemed, from the one they had just left.

Puzzled and wishing to see more of his surroundings, Tom lighted a match. He dropped it with a startled exclamation.

"Stand back, Ruth! Get behind me!"

"What's the rumpus?" a voice drawled behind them. The boys were crowding into the cave. "Think you see somethin', mister?"

"Bears!" replied Tom grimly. "Two of them!"

CHAPTER 25

SUNLIGHT ONCE MORE

Somewhere some one laughed nervously. Another struck a match. Ruth was crowded back into a corner behind Tom's broad shoulders.

In the flickering light of more matches she stared out from her enforced retirement upon the queerest tableau she had ever seen. Curiously enough, she was not frightened. It all seemed so unreal, fantastic.

Cowboys all around, their weary, white faces lit up oddly by the flickering light, every one with a hand on his holster, quiet, tense, and in the far corner of the place, backed up against the wall, two great, clumsy animals staring at the intruders with eyes half frightened, half fierce!

Even as Ruth stared, fascinated, one of them growled and moved forward a clumsy step. The other, as though encouraged by the defiance of its mate, growled also and ambled forward.

A bear is always more apt to run than fight. But, trapped here in the narrow confines of the cave with a certainty of attack from the rear should they try to escape, the bears took the only course left open to them—battle with their enemies. And a bear, roused to the attack, is a formidable foe!

As the great menacing beasts lunged forward the last feeble match went out, leaving the place in darkness. Only the faint ray of light from the far end of the cave mitigated the intense gloom.

Ruth shrank closer to Tom. The hair began to rise on her tingling scalp. She *was* frightened now!

She heard the muttered remarks of the cowboys.

"If we all fire we'll get one of 'em."

"Leave it to Cameron and me, we're nearest!" Layton Boardman's voice was clear and sharp. "Over against the light, Cameron—can you see?"

The bears had halted, probably nonplussed for a moment by the failure of the light that had so clearly shown them their enemies.

One of them, a huge lump of shadow, bulked against the faint light from the opening.

Tom grunted. With a roar, the shadow moved forward.

There was a shot! Another!

"Got him!" was Boardman's exultant cry.

But the gray shadow against the light, halted with a grunt of surprise as Tom's first bullet grazed his huge shoulder, now lumbered forward again, moving with incredible swiftness.

Ruth, cowering behind Tom, felt rather than saw the nearness of the brute, knew that it had reared and was towering above them!

Tom's pistol cracked again and then again.

The sinister shadow reeled, wavered, and fell, raking Tom's arm in the descent, tearing the skin from shoulder to wrist.

Ruth was vaguely aware that other matches were being struck and in the weird light saw the faces of men bending eagerly above two great beasts, one of which still kicked feebly.

Ruth's hand, falling on Tom's arm, came away hot and sticky. She saw then the rent in his coat and the blood dripping from his fingers.

"Tom, you're hurt! Oh, Tom, your arm!"

"It's nothing." Tom's voice was impatient, curt. "Lucky he didn't get more of us!"

But Layton Boardman had seen Tom's injury, as had some of the other boys.

"What you need, Cameron, is something to stop that blood," the former decided. "Come on, boys, let's get out of here. The sooner the better!"

All pressed forward.

Tom forced himself to walk steadily, though his arm throbbed badly and he was feeling dizzy.

Ruth put his arm across her shoulders and whispered to him to lean on her.

"You were wonderful, Tom!" she said. "I'm so proud of you!" The words went a long way toward keeping Tom's head up.

They found the opening of the cave larger than they had expected. It was an easy matter, once they had found their way over the bodies of the dead bears, to crawl out through the aperture into the blessed fresh air.

They stood silent for a moment, all of them, filling their lungs gratefully, faces upturned to the dazzling blue of the sky—a sky, but a short time before, they had thought never to see again!

Boardman looked at Tom, who was keeping his feet only by a tremendous effort of will.

"You must have come to pretty close quarters with that bear," he remarked gravely.

Tom nodded.

"If I had finished him with the first shot, like you," he said, "I wouldn't have been left—this—little—souvenir—" Then he crumpled up, his face a ghastly gray, the blood from his wounded arm reddening the ground where he lay.

Boardman started to lift him, but Ruth motioned him away.

"We have to stop that bleeding first," she said quietly, but with drawn lips. "He has lost far too much blood already."

While the men stood about, Ruth tore strips from her skirt, which as "Ann Marks," the heroine of the play, she fortunately wore, and tied them together. It was the matter of a moment to tear away the tattered sleeve of Tom's shirt; to twist the strip from the skirt around the arm above the wound and just beneath the shoulder.

Even then, twist with all her might, Ruth could not stop the spurting blood.

"Get me a stick somebody—quick!" she cried. "A little one that I can get through this knot!"

One of the boys was quick to see what she wanted and brought a slender, tough twig and handed it to her.

"Maybe this'll help, ma'am."

"Just the thing, thanks," returned Ruth.

She worked the twig beneath the bandage then began to twist it tighter and tighter until it seemed that the tourniquet must cut into the flesh.

But it worked! The blood flowed more and more sluggishly until finally it stopped altogether. Only then Ruth looked up, flushed and weary, but triumphant.

"Take him to the others as soon as you can, please," she directed. "He must have a doctor at once."

When, a few moments later, the disheveled band appeared before their would-be rescuers, bearing Tom among them, those digging at the débris stared for a moment as though they saw a band of ghosts.

But only for a moment. Then such a reunion, such a laughing and shouting and crying hysteria of welcome ensued as that grim old mountain had never witnessed before.

"Now that I've got you again, I'm never going to let you go," Helen cried, clinging to Ruth.

"We must get Tom to the ranch at once—at once, Helen! He may die—"

"Tommy boy!" All the color swept out of Helen's face.

Tom did not die, though the doctor declared Ruth's improvised tourniquet had much to do with that result.

"It was quick work and thorough, my dear," said the old doctor, eying Ruth benevolently over his thick-rimmed glasses. "I congratulate you."

But Ruth, turning away with the happy tears flooding to her eyes, did not need congratulations. All she cared for was the tremendous fact that Tom would live. Not only that, but he recovered with surprising speed and was out of bed in a day's time, though, of course, the wound was a much longer time in healing.

As soon as Ruth could bring herself around to thought of her picture again, the cameramen assured her that, so far from the scene being ruined by the second and unplanned landslide, it had been immeasurably strengthened.

"Nothing like the real thing to add realism to a film," one of them jovially informed her. "I believe the avalanches, artificial and real, will make the greatest picture ever filmed!"

Ruth's heart leaped at this.

"Some good seems to come even from the worst happenings," she said. "I'm glad that you had the presence of mind to keep on grinding!"

"We thought the whole thing was staged at first," they confessed to her. "And when we found out the true state of the case it was too late to stop grinding. The scene was shot."

"Glory be!" laughed Ruth, and went off to find Tom, Tom swathed in bandages but with the glamour of a wounded hero about him, nevertheless.

A day or two later Chess Copley came to Golden Pass. He had meant to surprise Helen, and his intention was certainly successful.

He came from the railroad station on horseback and when Helen recognized him she flung herself with such fervor at the rider that his mount became frightened and nearly ran away with him.

"That's the kind of a welcome I like!" cried Chess, as he dismounted and threw the reins to the grinning Andy. "Come here, fiancée, and receive the salute!"

Whereupon he kissed her quite heartily and openly before them all.

"How about business?" Helen asked him eagerly as she led him toward the porch. "You look as though you might be the bearer of good news—"

"The very best," replied Chess. "Business is great! Nothing now stands between us and eternal bliss. Hello!" as he caught sight of Tom, bandaged but grinning delightedly, "who threw a brick at you, son?"

Of course a recital of the tremendous events of the past few days was quickly poured into his interested ears.

"What did you do with the bears?" Chess queried when they came to the fight in the cave.

"The boys went back the next day and got them," Tom answered. "I reckon," with a grin, "they'll be eating bear meat for a week."

"Ugh!" said Ruth with a shudder, as she looked at Tom's arm, "I don't see how they could touch it!"

A delightful few days followed, during which Ruth added the finishing touches to her picture. There remained the final scene, the close-up of Layton Boardman and Ruth in the humble cabin of Ann Marks, the two lovers reunited and looking toward a rosy future.

It was a short time after the completion of this final scene that Tom found himself alone with Layton Boardman.

Poor Tom did not feel in the best of good humor, for that last scene in which Boardman had held Ruth close and kissed her still rankled in his mind.

"By gosh, I'm glad that last scene is shot," remarked the actor, with a sigh of relief. "I make a rotten lover, don't I, Cameron?"

"What? Rotten lover?" queried Tom. "What do you mean, Boardman?"

"Just what I said. I can't make love for a cent, no matter how I try. You see, it simply isn't in me. I don't care for girls that way—never did, no matter how hard they rave over me in the pictures."

"You—er—did it very well," stammered Tom. He was so astonished he scarcely knew what to say.

"Thanks for saying that. Then I won't have to do it all over again!" and Tom felt the note of relief in Boardman's voice. "I was afraid it might be necessary and that Miss Fielding would call me down for being such a wooden man at it. Ever since I agreed to take the part I tried to drill myself in it. And, believe me, drilling opposite to such a girl as Viola was some job! It went easier with Miss Fielding, but still, as I said before, I'm no lady's man and never was. I'd never give 'em a second hoot if it wasn't all a part of the job." And then Boardman strolled off to join some of the cowboys.

Tom stood stock still for a moment, gazing after the retreating moving picture actor. Then slowly a grin swept over his face.

"Tom Cameron, did you hear that?" he muttered to himself. "Never cared for any girl, never was a lady's man! 'Drilled myself in it!' Gosh, and I thought it was all real! Well, I've been seven kinds of a fool—I'll say so myself!"

Some time later that same evening Tom asked Ruth what she meant to do about him now that she had finished her picture. She succeeded in putting him off once more, though this time without hurting his feelings.

"Wait just a little while, Tommy-boy," she pleaded. "Just till I see myself on the screen. I must first know what kind of an actress I make."

It was not very long after this that Ruth found her new picture advertised in electric lights before one of the big moving picture houses in New York.

The first few scenes in which Ruth appeared were sufficient to convince those critics of the moving picture world who had gathered to view "Hearts of the Mountains" that a new and scintillating star had appeared on the horizon.

It is not often that one finds author, director, and star all in the person of one charming girl. Ruth's career was unique enough to satisfy even the most enthusiastic searchers after romance.

The avalanche was a tremendous spectacle. Those in the theater, gripped and stirred by the power of it, rose as a man and demanded the appearance of the author of the play.

Ruth, who was in the audience, was lifted to the stage by the eager hands of her admirers.

Flushed, tremulous, but wholly in command of herself, she said a few words of appreciation. The last part of her impromptu little speech was fairly drowned beneath the thunderous wave of applause that swept the theater.

Ruth knew that, in that moment, she had won fame.

Sol Bloomberg's sly attempt to punish Ruth for her acquisition of Boardman and, by stealing Viola, to make a failure of Ruth's picture had come to worse than nothing.

His picture, starring Viola and her lover, Tony Martano, was a disastrous failure. No one seemed to know just why—except perhaps Bloomberg himself. At any rate, one "listening in" for a moment on a conversation held between him and one of his directors, might possibly have found a clew to the mystery.

"It ain't that Viola ain't a good actress, Jim," the picture magnate asseverated, chewing viciously upon a huge and unlighted cigar. "It's just that she's plum silly over that Dago she's fell for."

The director nodded in deep dejection.

"Don't you suppose I know it? She lets Tony Martano hog all her best scenes. And he's some ham actor! I tell you, Sol," he went on with a frankness born of long and intimate association, "you sure pulled a bone when you put them two in the same picture."

Bloomberg flared up at this.

"I wouldn't 'a' got Viola at all if I hadn't held Tony out as bait. You know that as well as I do. Now keep still and get out! I gotta think!"

That his thoughts were not pleasant ones was proved a few moments later when he slammed his hat down on his head and angrily left the office, the mangled cigar, unlit, still between his teeth.

There were more reasons than one for Bloomberg's deep depression. Not only had he lost money through the failure of his picture, but what shreds of reputation remained to him, as well.

The story of how he had tempted Ruth's star into breaking her contract had gone the rounds as such bits of scandal will in the moving picture world. Ruth was applauded for her courage and resource, while Bloomberg became a laughing stock even among those he called his friends. Nor were

Viola's chances for making a good contract helped by her desertion of the Fielding Film Corporation at a critical time.

Ruth would not have been human had she failed to gloat a little over the downfall of her enemies.

"So are the wicked punished!" she said, with a twinkle in her eyes, to Helen.

They were back in the living room of the old house at the Red Mill.

At this observation of her chum Helen looked up and laughed affectionately, albeit still with that faint touch of envy.

"You lucky, lucky girl!" she murmured. "With the world at your feet, to say nothing of Tom!"

THE END